His blue gaze met hers, direct and powerful. "How long *has* it been?"

"Has it been for what?"

"Since you've been out on a date?"

Sam took such a deep sip of water she nearly drowned. "I could ask you the same thing."

"My answer's easy. A week."

"Oh." She put the glass down. "I thought you said you didn't have that much free time."

"I was exaggerating. I'm a writer." That grin again. "Given to hyperbole and all that."

Was he…flirting with her? Was that why everything within her seemed touched with fever? Why her stomach couldn't stop flip-flopping? Why she alternately wanted to run—and to stay?

It was simply because he was right. She hadn't been out on a date in forever. She wasn't used to this kind of head-on attention from a man. Especially a man as good at the head-on thing as he was.

"So which would you rather?" Flynn asked. "A date? Or an interview?"

The interview, her mind urged. *Say interview.* The business. The ba̶̶̶̶̶̶̶̶̶̶̶̶̶̶̶̶̶̶̶̶ revenue. Her person̶̶̶̶̶̶̶̶̶̶̶̶̶̶̶̶̶̶̶̶ always had. The busi̶̶̶̶̶̶̶̶̶̶̶̶̶̶̶̶̶̶̶̶

"A date."

Dear Reader

Christmas. Is there a more magical time of year? To me, it's the season of miracles. Of possibilities. In the Midwest, where I live, the first snowfall of the year is as eagerly awaited as Santa's arrival. Though I'm more than done with the cold weather by the middle of January, the entire month of December seems like something almost otherworldly when those first flakes start to drift to the ground.

A major part of the holiday for me is the food. I love to cook (which is why my blog at www.shirleyjump.blogspot.com is all about food!), and through the holiday season I'm cooking pretty much non-stop. Cookies, breads, stews— you name it, I'm making it. I get the kids involved, and not only serve the food to my family, but share a lot of it with my friends, too (and, hey, that keeps me from gaining all that weight!).

So it seemed appropriate to write a book that featured holiday food, and I wrapped that story with the magical theme of Christmas and the possibility of love. I hope you enjoy Sam and Flynn's story, and if you have a moment between the gift-wrapping and mugs of hot cocoa, drop me an e-mail at shirley@shirleyjump.com and share your favourite moment from the story!

Wishing you all the best this holiday season

Shirley

MARRY-ME CHRISTMAS

BY
SHIRLEY JUMP

MILLS & BOON®
Pure reading pleasure™

First published in Great Britain 2008
Harlequin Mills & Boon Limited,
Eton House, 18-24 Paradise Road, Richmond, Surrey TW9 1SR

© Shirley Kawa-Jump, LLC 2008

ISBN: 978 0 263 86558 5

Set in Times Roman 13 on 14 pt
02-1208-50984

Printed and bound in Spain
by Litografia Rosés, S.A., Barcelona

New York Times bestselling author **Shirley Jump** didn't have the will-power to diet, nor the talent to master under-eye concealer, so she bowed out of a career in television and opted instead for a career where she could be paid to eat at her desk—writing. At first, seeking revenge on her children for their grocery store tantrums, she sold embarrassing essays about them to anthologies. However, it wasn't enough to feed her growing addiction to writing funny. So she turned to the world of romance novels, where messes are (usually) cleaned up before The End. In the worlds Shirley gets to create and control, the children listen to their parents, the husbands always remember holidays, and the housework is magically done by elves. Though she's thrilled to see her books in stores around the world, Shirley mostly writes because it gives her an excuse to avoid cleaning the toilets and helps feed her shoe habit. To learn more, visit her website at www.shirleyjump.com

Praise for Shirley Jump...

About *NYT* bestselling anthology *Sugar and Spice*:
'Jump's office romance gives the collection a kick, with fiery writing.'
—*PublishersWeekly.com*

'Shirley Jump always succeeds in getting the plot, the characters, the settings and the emotions right.'
—*CataRomance.com*

'Shirley Jump begins *The Wedding Planners* with SWEETHEART LOST AND FOUND. It's smart, funny, and quite moving at times, and the characters have a lot of depth.'
—*Romantic Times BOOKreviews*

A Bride
for all Seasons

Would your perfect wedding be in **spring**,
when flowers are starting to blossom and it's the
perfect season for new beginnings…?

Or perhaps a balmy garden wedding
set off by a riot of colour that makes the **summer** bride
glow with the joys of a happy future…?

Do you dream of being an **autumn** bride,
walking down the aisle amid the dazzling reds
and burnished golds of falling leaves?

Or of a **winter** wedding dusted with
glistening white snowflakes, celebrated by
the ringing of frosty church bells…?

With Mills & Boon® Romance you can have them all!
And best of all you can experience the rush of
falling in love with a gorgeous groom…

In April we celebrated spring, with:
THE BRIDE'S BABY
by **Liz Fielding**

In June:
SAYING YES TO THE MILLIONAIRE
by **Fiona Harper**

In September:
THE MILLIONAIRE'S PROPOSAL
by **Trish Wylie**

Don't miss Christmas wedding bells this month:
MARRY-ME CHRISTMAS
by **Shirley Jump**

Visit http://abrideforallseasons.blogspot.com
to find out more…

CHAPTER ONE

FLYNN MACGREGOR hated Riverbend, Indiana, from the second his Lexus stalled at the single stop light in the quaint town center, right beneath the gaily decorated Christmas swags of pine needles and red bows. The entire snow-dusted town seemed like something out of a movie.

There were people walking to and fro with wrapped gifts, stores bedecked with holiday decorations, and even snowflakes, falling at a slow and steady pace, as if some set decorator was standing in the clouds with a giant shaker.

Okay, so *hated* might be a strong word. Detested, perhaps. Loathed. Either way, he didn't want to be here, especially when he'd been forced into the decision.

His editor at *Food Lovers* magazine had assigned him this story in Riverbend, knowing Flynn, of everyone on staff, could get the job done. Write an incisive, unique piece on the little bakery—a bakery rumored to have cookies that inspired people to fall in love, his editor had said. So here he was, spending the Christmas holiday holed up in the middle of nowhere penning one more of the stories that had made him famous.

Flynn scowled. He couldn't complain. Those stories had been his bread and butter forever, a very lucrative butter at that. And after that little fiasco in June, he needed to get his edge back, re-establish his position at the top of the writer pack. To do that, he'd do what he always did—suck it up, feign great joy at the festive spirit surrounding him and get to work.

Then he could get back to Boston, back to Mimi, and back to civilization. This town, with its Norman Rockwell looks, had to be as far from civilization as Mars was from Earth. Not that he had anything against quaint, but he lived in a world of iPods, e-mail and high-speed Internet connections. Riverbend looked like the kind of place that thought Bluetooth was a dental disease.

So, here he was, at the Joyful Creations Bakery.

Oh, joy.

He pushed his car to the side of the road, then grabbed his notebook and headed across the street. The crowd in front of the Joyful Creations Bakery blocked most of the plateglass window, but Flynn could see that storefront, too, had not been spared by the town's festive elves. A trio of lighted wreaths hung in the window, one of them even forming the *O* in the business's name.

"Nauseatingly cute," Flynn muttered under his breath.

He circumvented the line that stretched out the door, around the bakery and all the way to the corner of Larch Street. Ignoring the snow falling from the sky, couples stood together—most of the men looking none too keen on the idea of being dragged off to a bakery purported to be a food love source, while groups of women chatted excitedly about the "romance cookies."

It took sheer willpower for Flynn not to roll his eyes. The airline magazine that had first broken the story had clearly created an epidemic. By the time this piece hit *Food Lovers'* Valentine's Day issue, the shop would be overrun with the lovelorn. He hoped the owner was prepared for the onslaught. Flynn knew, from personal experience, how a too-fast rocket to success could be as destructive as a too-quick drop to the bottom.

Regardless, he was here to do a job, not offer a business consultation.

He brushed by a woman holding a toddler and entered Joyful Creations. A blast of warm air and holiday music greeted him like he'd jumped into a Christmas bath. The scent of fresh-baked bread, coupled with vanilla, cinnamon and a hint of raspberry, assaulted his senses. The waiting patrons were surely impressed, but Flynn had seen all this and smelled all this before.

"Hey, no cutting," the woman said.

"I'm not buying anything," he replied, and kept going. Get in, get the story, get out. Get back to Boston. Hopefully before Mimi even noticed he was gone. *If* Mimi even noticed he was gone.

"Why would you battle this crowd if you weren't going to buy anything?" the woman asked, shuffling the kid to the other hip.

"For..." Flynn turned toward the counter where two women were busy filling orders as quickly as they were being shouted over the din. One, gray-haired and petite, the other, tall and blond, curvy, with the kind of hips that said she didn't spend her days obsessing over having two pieces of celery or one.

Wow. The airline magazine hadn't run a photo of Samantha Barnett with their story, just one of the cookies. But clearly, she was the owner that the writer had described as "energetic, friendly, youthful."

"Her," Flynn said.

"Sam? Good luck with that." The woman laughed, then turned back to her kid, playing with his nose. Pretending the thing was a button or something. Flynn had no experience with other people's children and had no intention of starting now, so he moved away.

It took the navigational skills of a fleet admiral to wade through the crowd inside the shop, but a few minutes later, Flynn had managed to reach the glass counter. He stood to the far right, away from the line of paying customers, most of them looking like they'd come straight from placing a personal ad. "Are you Samantha Barnett?"

The blonde looked up. Little tendrils of her hair were beginning to escape her ponytail, as if the first few strands were thinking of making a break for the border. She wore little makeup, just a dash of red lip gloss and a dusting of mascara. He suspected the slight hint of crimson in her cheeks was natural, a flush from the frantic pace of the warm bakery. A long white apron with the words *Joyful Creations* scrolled across the middle in a curled red script hugged her frame, covering dark denim jeans and a soft green V-neck sweater. "I'm sorry, sir, you'll have to get into the line."

"I'm not here to buy anything."

That made her pause. Stop putting reindeer-shaped cookies into a white box. "Do you have a delivery or some mail for me?"

He shook his head. Vowed to buy a new dress coat, if he looked like a mailman in this one. "I just want to talk to you."

"Now is not a good time." She let out a little laugh. "I'm kind of busy."

"Yeah, well, I'm on a deadline." He fished a business card out of his pocket and slid it across the glass case. "Flynn MacGregor with *Food Lovers* magazine. Maybe you've heard of it?"

Her face lit up, as so many others before hers had. Everyone had heard of *Food Lovers*. It was *the* magazine about the food industry, carried in every grocery store and bookstore, read by thirty million people nationwide. A print mention in its pages was the equivalent of starring in a movie.

Even if *Food Lovers* magazine's focus had shifted, ever since Tony Reynolds had taken over as editor a year ago. His insistence on finding the story behind the story, the dish on every chef, restaurant and food business, had given the magazine more of a tabloid feel, but also tripled readership in a matter of months.

At first, Flynn hadn't minded doing what Tony wanted. But as each story became more and more invasive of people's personal lives, Flynn's job had begun to grate on him. More than once he had thought about quitting. But Flynn MacGregor hadn't gotten to where he was by turning tail just because he butted heads with an editor or ran into a roadblock ot two.

"Wow," Samantha said, clearly not bothered by

Food Lovers' reputation. "You want to talk to me? What about?"

"Your bakery. Why you got into this business. What makes Joyful Creations special…" As he ran through his usual preinterview spiel, Flynn bit back his impatience. Reminded himself this was his four hundredth interview, but probably her first or second. Flynn could recite the questions without even needing to write them down ahead of time. Heck, he could practically write her answers for her. She got into baking because she loved people, loved food. The best part about being in business in a small town was the customers. Yada-yada-yada.

As for the cookies that made people fall in love, Flynn put no stock in things like that. He'd seen soups that supposedly made women go into labor, cakes that were rumored to jump-start diets, appetizers bandied about as the next best aphrodisiac. None of which had proven to be true, but still, the magazine had run a charming piece in its pages, appealing to its vast readership.

While he was here, he'd track down a few of the couples who owed their happiness to the sugar-and-flour concoctions, then put some kind of cutesy spin on the story. The art department would fancy up the headline with dancing gingerbread men or something, and they'd all walk away thinking Joyful Creations was the best thing to come along since Cupid and his trademark bow.

"That's pretty much how it works, Miss Barnett," Flynn finished, wrapping up his sugar-coated version of the article process.

The bakery owner nodded. "Sounds great. Relatively painless."

"Sam? I hate to interrupt," another woman cut in, just as Flynn was getting ready to ask his first question, "but I really need to pick up my order. I have a preschool waiting. And you know preschoolers. They want their sugar."

Samantha Barnett snapped to attention, back to her customer. "Oh, sure, Rachel. Sorry about that. Two dozen, right?"

The other woman, a petite brunette, grinned. "And one extra, for the teacher."

"Of course." Samantha smiled, finished putting the reindeer into the box, then tied it with a thin red ribbon and handed the white container across the counter. "Here you go."

"Will you put it on my tab?"

Samantha waved off the words. "Consider it a Christmas gift to the Bumblebees."

Not a smart way to run a business, giving away profits like that, but Flynn kept that to himself. He wasn't her financial consultant. "The interview, Miss Barnett?"

Behind them, the line groaned. Samantha

brushed her bangs off her forehead. "Can I meet with you later today? Maybe after the shop closes? I'm swamped right now."

She had help, didn't she? On top of that, he had somewhere else he wanted to go before beginning that long drive back to Boston, not endless amounts of time to wait around for preschoolers to get their sugar rush. "And I'm on deadline."

The next person had slipped into the space vacated by Miss Bumblebee, a tall senior citizen in a flap-eared flannel cap and a Carhartt jacket. He ambled up to the counter, leaned one arm on the glass case and made himself at home, like he was planning on spending an hour or two there. "Hiya, Samantha. Heard about the article in that airline magazine. Congratulations! You really put our town on the map, not that you weren't a destination from the start, what with those cookies and all." He leaned forward, cupping a beefy hand around his mouth. "Though I'm not so sure I want all these tourists to stay. They're causing quite the traffic jam."

Samantha chuckled. "Thanks, Earl. And sorry I can't do anything about the traffic. Except fill the orders as fast as I can." She slid a glance Flynn's way.

"You give me my interview, Miss Barnett, and I'll be out of your hair."

"Give me a few hours, Mr. MacGregor, and I'll give you whatever you want."

He knew there was no innuendo in her words, but the male part of him heard one all the same. He cleared his throat and took a step back. "I have to get back on the road. Today. So why don't you just cooperate with me and we can both be happy?"

"I have customers to wait on, and it looks like now you're going to have a long wait either way." She gestured toward the windows with her chin as her hands worked beneath the counter, shoveling muffins into a bag. "You might as well make yourself comfortable."

Flynn turned and looked through the glass. And saw yet another reason to hate Riverbend.

A blizzard.

By noon, Sam was already so exhausted, she was sure she'd collapse face-first into the double-layer cinnamon streusel. But she pasted a smile on her face, kept handing out cookies and pastries, all while dispensing directions to her staff. She'd called in her seasonal part-timers, and everyone else she could think of, right down to Mary, who did the weekend cleaning, to help keep up with the sudden influx of tourists. It seemed every person in a three-state area had read the article and turned out to see if Joyful

Creations would live up to its reputation of bringing love to people who tried Grandma Joy's Secret Recipe Cherry Chocolate Chunk Cookies.

Sam had long heard the rumors about her grandmother's cookies—after all, they were the very treats Grandma Joy had served to Grandpa Neil when they had first met—but had never quite believed all the people who credited the tiny desserts for their happy unions. Then a reporter from *Travelers* magazine had tried them on a trip through town and immediately fallen in love with one of the local women. The two of them had run off to Jamaica and gotten married the very next weekend. Afterward, the reporter had raved about the cookies and his happy ending in the airline publication, launching Sam's shop to national fame, and turning a rumor into a fact.

Ever since, things hadn't slowed down. Sam had worked a lot of hours before—but this was ridiculous. Nearly every spare moment was spent at the bakery, working, restocking and filling orders. But it was all for a larger goal, so she kept pushing, knowing the bigger reward was on the horizon.

"I can't decide." The platinum-blond woman, dressed head to toe in couture, put a leather-gloved finger to her lips. "How many calories did you say were in the peanut butter kiss cookies?"

The smile was beginning to hurt Sam's face. "About one hundred and ten per cookie."

"And those special cherry chocolate chunk ones?"

"About a hundred and fifty."

"Do those cookies really work? Those love ones?"

"That's what people say, ma'am."

"Well, it would really have to be worth the calories. That's a lot to work off in the gym, you know, if I don't meet Mr. Right. And if I meet Mr. Wrong—" the woman threw up her hands "—well that's even more time on the treadmill."

Sam bit her lip, then pushed the smile up further.

"Do you happen to know the fat grams? I'm on a very strict diet. My doctor doesn't want me to have more than twenty-two grams of fat per day."

From what Sam could see, the woman didn't have twenty-two grams of fat in her entire body, but she kept that to herself. "I don't know the grams of fat offhand, ma'am, but I assure you, none of these cookies have that many per serving."

The gloved finger to the lips again. She tipped her head to the right, then the left, her pageboy swinging with the indecision. Behind her, the entire line shifted and groaned in annoyance. "I still don't know."

"Why don't you buy one of each?" Sam said. "Have one today and one tomorrow."

"That's a wonderful idea." The woman beamed, as if Sam were Einstein. She handed her money across the glass case to Ginny while Sam wrapped the cookies in wax paper and slid them into a bright white Joyful Creations box, then tied a thin red ribbon around the box. "But…"

"But what?"

"How can I decide which one to have today?"

Sam just smiled, told the woman to have a merry Christmas, and moved on to the next customer. Four hundred of Grandma Joy's secret recipe cherry chocolate chunk cookies later, the line had finally thinned. Sam bent over, taking a moment to straighten the trays, whisk away a few crumbs and bring order back to the display.

Then, through the glass she glimpsed a pair of designer men's shoes, their glossy finish marred by road salt, dots of dried snow. Her gaze traveled upward. Pressed trousers, a dark gray cashmere dress coat. White shirt. Crimson tie.

He was back. Flynn MacGregor.

Blue eyes, so deep, so dark, they were the color of the sky when a thunderstorm came rolling through. Black, wavy hair that had been tamed with a close cut. And a face set in rigid stone. "I have waited. For hours. Watched dozens of customers come through here, thinking you have the answer to love, marriage and apparently the beginnings of the earth." He let out a breath of displeasure. "I had no idea you could get such bonuses with your coffee cake."

His droll manner told her it wasn't a joke, nor a compliment. "I don't purport to offer anything other than baked goods, Mr. MacGregor."

"That's not what the people in that line thought. That very *long* line, I might add. One that took nearly three hours to clear out. And now—" he flicked out a wrist and glanced at his watch "—I'm never going to get to where I needed to go today if I don't get this interview done. Now."

"I don't think you're going to be able to make it farther than a few miles. I doubt the roads are clear. The weather is still pretty bad."

"My editor is from the mailman school of thought. Neither blizzard nor earthquake shall stop a deadline."

She eyed him. "And I take it you agree with his philosophy?"

"I didn't get to where I am in my career by letting a little snow stop me." He leaned forward. "So, do you have time *now*, Miss Barnett?"

Clearly, Sam's best bet was to fit in with his plans. Business had slowed enough for her to give the reporter some time anyway. "Sure. And it'd be great to sit down for a minute." Sam turned toward her great-aunt. "Aunt Ginny, could you handle the counter for a little while?"

The older woman gave her a grin. "Absolutely."

Sam pivoted back to Flynn. The man was handsome enough, even if he was about as warm and fuzzy as a hedgehog. But, he had come all the way from Boston, and Lord knew she could use the publicity. The airline magazine story had been a great boon, but Sam was a smart enough business person to know that kind of PR wouldn't last long. "Can I get you some coffee? A Danish? Muffin? Cookies?"

"I'd like a sampling of the house specialties. And some coffee would be nice."

He had good looks, but he had all the friendliness of a brick wall. His words came out clear, direct, to the point. No wasted syllables, no wide smiles.

Nevertheless, he offered the one gift Sam had been dreaming about for years. A positive profile of the bakery in the widely popular *Food Lovers* magazine would be just the kickoff she needed to launch the new locations she'd been hoping to open this year. Heck, the exposure she'd hoped and prayed for ever since she'd taken over the bakery. Coupled with the boost in business the airline magazine's story had given her, Joyful Creations was on its way to nationwide prominence.

And she was on her way out of Riverbend.

Finally.

Not to mention, she'd also have the financial security she needed to fund her grandmother's long-term care needs. It was all right here.

In Flynn MacGregor. If that didn't prove Santa existed, Sam wasn't sure what did.

She hummed snippets of Christmas carols as she filled a holly-decorated plate with a variety of the bakery's best treats. Gingerbread cookies, pecan bars, cranberry orange muffins, white mocha fudge, peppermint chocolate bark, frosted sugar Santa cookies—she piled them all on until the plate threatened to spill.

"Don't forget some of these," Ginny said, handing Sam a couple cherry chocolate chunk cookies.

"Aunt Ginny, I don't think he needs—"

"He came here for the story about the special cookies, didn't he?" Her great-aunt gave her a wide smile. "And if the stories are true, you never know what might happen if he takes a bite."

"You don't seriously believe—"

"I do, and you should, too." Ginny wagged a finger. "Why, your grandmother and grandfather never would have fallen in love if not for this recipe. I wouldn't have married your Uncle Larry if it hadn't been for these cookies. Why, look at all the proof around you in this town. You just don't believe in them because you've never tried them."

"That's because I'm too busy baking to eat."

Sam sighed, accepted the two cookies and added them to the plate. What was the harm, really? There was nothing to that legend. Regardless of what Aunt Ginny thought.

Balancing the plate, Sam crossed the room and placed the treats and a steaming mug of coffee before the reporter. "Here you are, Mr.—"

And she lost the next word. Completely forgot his name.

He had taken off his coat and was sitting at one of the small round café tables in the corner, by the plate-glass windows that faced the town square. He had that air about him of wealth, all in the telltale signs of expensive fabric, perfectly fitting clothing, the way he carried himself. His sleeves were rolled up, exposing defined, muscled hands and forearms, fingers long enough to play piano, touch a woman and—

Whoa. She was staring.

"Mr. MacGregor," she finished. Fast. "Enjoy." Sam took a couple steps back. "Uh, enjoy."

He turned to her and a grin flashed across his face so quickly, she could have almost sworn she'd imagined it. But no, it had been there. A thank-you, perhaps. Or maybe amusement at her discomfit?

Either way, his smile changed his entire face. Softened his features. Made Sam's pulse race in a way it hadn't in a long time.

"You already said that," he said.

Okay, it had been amusement. Now she was embarrassed.

"Did I? Sorry. You, ah, make me nervous." No way would she admit public humiliation.

"I do? Why?"

"I haven't had a real reporter in the shop before. Well, except for Joey from the *Riverbend Times*, but that doesn't count. He's nineteen and still in college, and he's usually just here to get a cup of decaf because regular coffee makes him so hyper he can hardly write." She was babbling. What was wrong with her? Samantha Barnett never babbled. Never got unnerved.

Way to make a first impression, Sam.

"I should get back in the kitchen," Sam said, thumbing in that direction.

"I need to interview you. Remember? And I'd prefer not to shout my questions."

Now she'd annoyed him. "All right. Let me grab a cup of coffee. Unlike Joey, I *do* need the caffeine."

He let out a laugh. Okay, so it had been about a half a syllable long, but still, Sam took that as a good sign. A beginning. If he liked her and liked the food, maybe this Flynn guy would write a kick-butt review, and all her Christmas wishes would be granted.

But as she walked away, he started drumming his fingers on the table, tapping out his impatience one digit at a time.

Ginny tapped her on the shoulder when she reached the coffeepot. "Sam, I forget to mention something earlier."

"If it's about getting me to share Grandma's special recipe cookies with a man again—"

"No, no, it's about that magazine he's with. He said *Food Lovers*, didn't he?"

Sam poured some coffee into a mug. "Yes. It's huge. Everybody reads it, well, except for me. I never get time to read anything."

Ginny made a face. "Well, I read it, or at least I used to. Years ago, *Food Lovers* used to just be about food, you know, recipes and things like that, but lately, it's become more…"

"More what?" Sam prompted.

Her aunt paused a moment longer, then let out a breath. "Like those newspapers you see in the checkout stand. A lot of the stories are about the personal lives of the people who own the restaurants and the bakeries, not the food they serve. It's kind of…intrusive."

"What's wrong with writing stories about the people who own the businesses?"

Ginny shrugged. "Just be careful," she said, laying a hand on Sam's. "I know how you guard your privacy, and your grandmother's. I might not agree with your decision, but you're my niece, so I support you no matter what."

Sam drew Aunt Ginny into a hug. "Thank you."

"Anything for you, Sam," she said, then drew back. She glanced over the counter at Flynn MacGregor. "There's one other thing you need to be careful of, too."

"What's that?"

Ginny grinned. "He's awfully cute. That could be the kind of trouble you've been needing, dear niece, for a long time."

Sam grabbed her coffee mug. "Adding a relationship into my life, as busy as it is?" She shook her head. "That would be like adding way too much yeast to a batter. In the end, you get nothing but a mess."

CHAPTER TWO

SAM RETURNED with her coffee, Aunt Ginny's words of wisdom still ringing in her head, and slipped into the opposite seat from Flynn MacGregor. He had a pad of paper open beside him, turned to a blank page, with a ready pen. He'd sampled the coffee, but none of the baked goods. Not so much as a crumb of Santa's beard on the frosted sugar cookies. Nary a bite from Grandma's special cookies—the ones he'd presumably come all this way to write about.

Sam's spirits fell, but she didn't let it show. Maybe he wanted to talk to her first. Or maybe he was, as Aunt Ginny had cautioned, here solely for the story behind the bakery.

Her story.

"Are you ready *now?*" he asked.

"Completely."

"Good. Tell me the history of the bakery."

Sam folded her hands on the table. "Joyful

Creations was opened in 1948 by my grandmother Joy and grandfather Neil Barnett. My grandmother was an amazing cook. She made the most incredible cookies for our family every holiday. I remember one time I went over to her house, and she had 'invent a cookie' day. She just opened her cabinets, and she and I—"

"The bakery, Miss Barnett. Can we stick to that topic?"

"Oh, yes. Of course." Sam wanted to kick herself. Babbling again. "My grandfather thought my grandmother was so good, she should share those talents with Riverbend. So they opened the bakery."

He jotted down the information as she talked, his pen skimming across the page in an indecipherable scrawl.

Sam leaned forward. "Are you going to be able to read that later?"

He looked up. "This? It's my own kind of shorthand. No vowels, abbreviations only I know for certain words."

She chuckled. "It's like my recipes. Some of them have been handed down for generations. My grandmother never really kept precise records and some of them just say 'pecs' or 'CC.' They're like a puzzle."

He arched a brow. "Pecs? CC?"

"Pecans. And CC was shorthand for chocolate

chips." Sam smiled. "It took me weeks to figure out some of them, after I took over the bakery. I should have paid more attention when I was little."

His brows knitted in confusion. "I read it was a third-generation business. What happened to the second generation?"

"My parents died in a car accident when I was in middle school. I went to live with my grandparents. Grandpa Neil died ten years ago." Sam splayed her palms on the table and bit her lip. Flynn MacGregor didn't need to know more than that.

"And your grandmother? Is she still alive?"

Sam hated lying. It wasn't in her nature to do so. But now she was in a position where telling the truth opened a bucket of worms that could get out of hand. "She is, but no longer working in the bakery."

He wrote that down. "I'd like to interview her, too."

"You can't."

Flynn looked up. "Why?"

"She's…ill." That was all he needed to know. Joy's privacy was her own. This reporter could keep the story focused on the present.

Nevertheless, he made a note, a little note of mmm-hmm under his breath. Sam shifted in her chair. "Don't you want to try a cranberry orange muffin?"

"In a minute."

"But—"

"I'm writing an article, Miss Barnett, not a review."

She shifted some more. Maybe her unease stemmed from his presence. The airline magazine had done the interview part over the phone. The reporter had come in and bought some cookies, then found his happy ending, unbeknownst to Sam, at a different time. Talking to someone she couldn't see, and answering a few quick questions, had been easy. This face-to-face thing was much more difficult.

More distracting. Because this reporter had a deep blue, piercing gaze.

The bell over the door jingled and a whoosh of cold air burst into the room. "Sam!"

"Mrs. Meyers, how can I help you?"

"I need more cookies. My dog ate the box I brought home. I didn't even get a chance to feed the batch I bought to my Carl and that man is in the grumpiest of moods." Eileen Meyers swung her gaze heavenward. "He's hanging the Christmas lights."

"In this weather?"

"You know my husband. The man is as stubborn as a tick on a hunting dog, Sam. There are days I wonder why I'm even buying those cookies."

"Because they're your husband's favorites," Sam reminded her. Eileen had been in the day before, plunked down her money, her love for her husband still clear, even in a marriage that had celebrated its silver anniversary, and was edging its way toward gold.

Eileen harrumphed, but a smile played at the edge of her lips. "Will you get me another dozen?"

"Ginny can help you, Mrs. Meyers."

Eileen laid a hand on Sam's arm, her brown eyes filled with entreaty. "I love your Aunt Ginny, Sam, I do, but you know my Carl better than I do some days. He says you're the only one who can pick out the cookies he likes best."

Across from her, Flynn MacGregor's pen tapped once against his notepad. A reminder of where her attention should be.

"Please, Sam?" Eileen's hand held tight to Sam's arm. "It'll mean the world to Carl."

"This will just take a minute," she told Flynn. "Is that all right?"

"Of course." A smile as fake as the spray-paint snow on the windows whipped across his face. "I've already waited for that massive line of customers to go down. Dealt with my car breaking down, and a blizzard blowing through town, which has undoubtedly delayed my leaving, too. What's one more box of cookies?"

Sam filled Eileen's order as quickly as she could, trying to head off Eileen's attempts at conversation. And failing miserably. Eileen was one of those people who couldn't buy a newspaper without engaging in a rundown of her life story. By the time she had paid for her cookies, she'd told Sam—again—all about how she and Mr. Meyers had met, what he'd done to sweep her off her feet and how he'd lost his romantic touch long ago.

"Are you done playing advice columnist?" Flynn asked when Eileen finally left.

"I'm sorry. Things have been especially crazy here since word got out about those cookies." Sam gestured toward the plate, where the trio of Grandma's special recipe still sat, untouched.

"The ones that are purported to make people fall in love?"

She shrugged. "That's what people say."

"I take it you don't believe the rumors?"

She laughed. "I don't know. Maybe it's true. If two people find a happy ending because they eat my grandmother's cookies, then I think it's wonderful. For them, and for business."

Flynn arched a brow. "Happy endings? Over cookies?"

"Not much of a romantic, are you?"

"No. I'm a practical man. I do my job, and I don't dabble in all this—" he waved his hand "—fanciful stuff."

"Me, too." Sam laughed, the chuckle escaping her with a nervous clatter. "Well, not the man part."

"Of course." He nodded.

What was with this guy? He was as serious as a wreath without any decorations. Sam laced her fingers together and tried to get comfortable in the chair, but more, under his scrutiny. The sooner this interview was over, the better. "What else did you need to know?"

"How long have you been working here?"

"All my life. Basically, ever since I could walk. But I took over full-time when I was nineteen."

Surprise dropped his jaw. "Nineteen? Isn't that awfully young? What kind of business person could you be at that age?"

"You do what have to, Mr. MacGregor." She sipped at her coffee, avoiding his piercing gaze. He had a way of looking at a woman like he could see right through her. Like Superman's X-ray vision, only he wasn't looking at the color of her underwear, but at the secrets of her soul.

She pushed the plate closer to him. "I think you'd really like the sugar frosted cookies. They're a Joyful Creations specialty."

Again, he bypassed the plate in front of him, in favor of his notes. "Did you go to culinary school?"

She shook her head. "I couldn't. I was working here. Full-time."

"Having no life, you mean."

She bristled. "I enjoy my job."

"I'm sure you do." He flipped a page on his notepad, bringing him to a clean sheet of paper.

"What's that supposed to mean?"

"I'm not here to tell you how to run your business."

"And yet, you're judging me and you hardly know me."

Flynn folded his hands over his pad. "Miss Barnett, I've been covering this industry for a long time. Talked to hundreds of bakers and chefs. This is the kind of business that consumes you." He let out a laugh, another short, nearly bitter sound that barely became a full chuckle. "Pun intended."

"My business doesn't consume me." But as the words left her mouth, she knew Joyful Creations had, indeed, done that very thing, particularly in the last few weeks. The business had taken away her weekends. Vacations. Eaten up friendships, nights out, dates. Left her with this empty feeling, as if she'd missed a half of herself.

The half that had watched her friends grow up. Get married. Start families. While she had toiled in the bakery, telling herself there'd be time down the road. As one year passed, then two, then five, and Sam hit twenty-five, and tried not to tell herself she'd missed too much already. She had plenty of time—down the road.

There was a reason she worked so hard. A very important reason. And once she'd reached her goals, she'd take time off.

She would.

"I watched you earlier. And I've watched you as you've talked about this business. I can see the stars in your eyes," he went on. "The *Travelers'* magazine article has probably put the lofty idea in your head that you can become the next McDonald's or Mrs. Fields Cookies."

"It hasn't," Sam leapt to say, then checked her defensive tone. "Well, maybe a little. Did you see those lines? It's been that way nonstop for two weeks. I'm sure you've seen many businesses that became mega-successes after something like that. Don't you think it's possible for me to hit the big time?"

"I have seen it happen," he conceded. "And let me be the first to warn you to be careful what you wish for."

She leaned back in her chair and stared at him, incredulous. Ever since she'd met him, he'd been nothing but grouchy, and now here he was, trying to tell her how to run her own company. "Who put coal in your stocking this morning?"

"I'm just being honest. I believe in calling the shots I see."

"So do I, Mr. MacGregor," Sam said, rising. If she didn't leave this table in the next five seconds, she'd be saying things to this man that she didn't want to see in print. "And while we're on the subject of our respective industries, I think yours has made you as jaded and as bitter as a bushel of lemons." She gestured toward his still-full plate, and frustration surged inside her. With the busy day, with him, and especially with his refusal to try the very baked goods he was writing about yet already judging. "Maybe you should have started with the cookies first. A little sugar goes a long way toward making people happy. And you, sir, could use a lot of that."

CHAPTER THREE

"WELL, I WAS WRONG."

Flynn bit back the urge to curse. "What do you mean, wrong?"

"I replaced the air filter. And it turned out, that wasn't it. That means, I was wrong." Earl Klein shrugged. "It happens." He put out his hands, as if that explained why Flynn's car was sitting inside Earl's Tire and Repair on a lift six feet off the ground, a jumble of parts scattered below.

"Did you fix it?" Flynn asked. Of all the people to end up with, Earl would have been Flynn's last choice. He had asked around once he left the bakery, and it turned out the hunting cap guy he'd seen earlier owned the closest garage to Flynn's broken-down car. Although, given how circular a conversation with Earl was turning out to be, Flynn was beginning to regret his choice.

Earl stared at Flynn like he had all the intelligence of a duck. "Does your car *look* fixed?"

"Well, no, but I was hoping—"

"Your fuel filter needs to be replaced. I usually have one for your model on hand, but used my last one yesterday. Damnedest thing, too. Paulie Lennox comes in here, his car was running fine, then all of a sudden—"

"I don't care about Paulie Lennox. I don't even know him."

"Oh, you'd know him if you see him. He's six foot seven. Tallest man in Riverbend. Sings in the church choir. Voice of an angel. Ain't that weird for a guy that big? Must have organ pipes in his chest."

Flynn gritted his teeth. "How long?"

"How long are his vocal cords? Damned if I know. I'm no doctor."

"No, I meant how long until my car is fixed?"

"Oh, that." Earl turned around and looked at the Lexus as if it might tell him. "Day. Maybe two. Gotta wait for the part. You know, 'cept for Paulie, we don't get many of those fancy-dancy cars in here. If you'da come in here with a Ford, or Chevy pickup, I'd have you fixed up a couple minutes. But this, well, this requires what we call special treatment."

Flynn hoped like hell this guy would give the Lexus special treatment, considering what the car cost. "Did you order the part? Or can you go get it?"

"I ordered it. Can't go get it."

Flynn wanted to bang his head into a brick wall. He'd probably get further in the conversation if he did. This was like playing Ping-Pong by himself. "Why can't you go get the part?"

Earl leaned in closer to Flynn. "Have you looked outside, son? It's *snowing*. Blizzard's on its way into town, hell, it's already here. Only an idiot would drive in this. And I'm no idiot."

Flynn would beg to differ. "It's four days before Christmas."

"That don't change the icy roads. Old Man Winter, he doesn't have the same calendar as you and me."

Flynn dug deep for more patience. "Is there another garage in town?"

Earl's face frowned in offense. "Now, I'm going to pretend you didn't even ask that, because you're from out of town. My garage is the best one for miles, and the only one."

Of course. Flynn groaned. "I have some place I need to go. As soon as possible."

That was if he even decided to make that stop in southern Indiana. On the drive out here from Boston, it had seemed like a good idea, but the closer Flynn got to the Midwest, the more he began to second-guess his impromptu decision. That was why he had yet to make any promises he couldn't keep. Better not to say a word. That way, no one was disappointed. Again.

"Well, that ain't happenin', is it?" Earl grinned. "You best get down to Betsy's Bed and Breakfast. She'll put you up and feed you, too." He patted his stomach. "That woman can cook. And she's real pretty, too. But she's spoken for. So don't go thinking you can ask her out. Me and Betsy, we have an understanding." Earl wiggled a shaggy gray brow. "Thanks to those cookies of Sam's, which helped us out a lot. Brought me and Betsy together, they did."

Flynn put up his hands, hoping to ward off the mental picture that brought up. "I don't want to know about it. Just point me in the general direction."

Thirty seconds later, Flynn was back outside, battling an increasingly more powerful wind. The snow had multiplied and six more inches of the thick wet stuff now coated the sidewalks. The earlier tourist crowds had apparently gotten the hint and left for their hotels or real cities. Traffic, what there was left in Riverbend, had slowed to a crawl. Within minutes, the damp snow had seeped through Flynn's shoes and he was slogging through slush, ruining five-hundred-dollar dress shoes. Damn it. What he wouldn't do for a sled dog team right now.

"Do you need a ride?"

He turned to see Samantha Barnett at the wheel of an older model Jeep Cherokee. Or what he thought was Samantha Barnett. She was bundled in a blue parka-type jacket that obscured most of her delicate features, the hood covering all of her blond hair. But the smile—that 100-watt smile he'd seen earlier in the bakery—that he could see.

Only a fool would say no to that. And to the dry, warm vehicle.

"Sure." He opened the door and climbed inside. Holiday music pumped from the stereo, filling the interior of the Jeep like stuffing in a turkey. Again, Flynn got that Norman Rockwell feeling. "Is this town for real?" he asked as Sam put the Jeep in gear and they passed yet another decorated window display—this one complete with a moving Santa's workshop.

"What do you mean?"

"It's a bit too jolly, don't you think? I mean, it's almost nauseating."

"Nauseating? It's Christmas. People are feeling…festive."

"Festive? In this?" He gestured out the window. "My feet are soaked, nearly frostbitten, I'm sure. My car is being worked on by the village idiot, I'm on a deadline that I can't miss and I'm being held hostage in a town that thinks Christmas is the be-all and end-all."

"Well, isn't it?"

"There are three hundred and sixty-four other days in the year, you know."

Sam stared at him. Never before had she met anyone with as little Christmas spirit as Flynn MacGregor. "Don't you celebrate Christmas? Put up a tree? Drink a little eggnog?"

Flynn didn't answer. Instead he glanced out the window. "Do you know a place called Betsy's Bed and Breakfast?"

"Of course I do. It's a small town. Everyone knows everyone else, and everything. You burn your toast in the morning and Mrs. Beedleman over on Oak Street is on your doorstep, lending you her toaster before lunch." Sam smiled. "I'm on my way to make a couple of deliveries, so I have time. Besides, driving you to Betsy's is the least I can do to say I'm sorry for being so short with you earlier." She took a left, using caution as she made the turn and navigated through the downtown intersection. "I guess I'm just a little protective when it comes to the bakery."

"Most business owners are." He kept watching out the window. "Is that a *live* reindeer I see in the park? This town is Christmas gone overboard."

She turned to him. "You're kind of grumpy, aren't you? This whole anti-Christmas thing, the way you jumped on me about my business... Grumpy."

He sat back. "No. Just...honest."

She shrugged. "I call it grumpy."

"Honest. Direct. To the point."

She flashed another glance his way. "You know who else was grumpy? Ebenezer Scrooge. Remember him? He got a pretty bad preview of his future."

Flynn rolled his eyes. "That was fiction. I'm talking real life."

"Uh-huh. Let me know when the ghost of Christmas Future comes knocking on your door."

"When he does, I'll know it's time to put away the scotch."

Samantha laughed. Her laughter had a light, musical sound to it. Like the holiday carols coming from the stereo. Flynn tried hard not to like the sound, but…

He did.

"Listen, you had a rough day," Sam said, "so you're excused for any and all grumpiness. And don't worry, you're in good hands with Earl."

Flynn let out a short gust of disbelief. "I'd be in better hands with a troop of baboons."

"Oh, Earl's not so bad. He's really easygoing. You just gotta get used to him. And, indulge him by listening to his stories once in a while. Nothing makes him happier than that. You might even get a discount on your service if you suffer through his account of the blizzard of '78 and how he baked a turkey, even though the power was out for four days." She shot him a grin.

"I don't have time for other people's stories."

"You're a reporter, isn't your whole mission to get the story?"

"Just the ones they pay me for." That pay had been lucrative, ever since he turned in his first article. Flynn had risen to the top of his field, becoming well-known in the magazine industry for being the go-to guy for getting the job done—on time, and right on the word count.

Then he'd hit a road bump, a big one, with the celebrity chef back in June. His editor had lost faith in Flynn, but worse—

Flynn had temporarily lost faith in himself.

He refused to get sucked into that emotional vortex again. He'd gotten to the top by staying out of the story, and he'd do that again here. Get in and out, as fast as possible.

And then make one stop, one very important stop, before heading back to Boston.

But he couldn't do either if he didn't shake off that silly whisper of conscience, write the story his editor wanted and get it in on time, no matter what it took.

The interior of the Jeep had reached a comfortable temperature and Sam pulled off one glove, then the other. Her hands, he noticed, were slim and delicate, the nails short and no-nonsense, not polished. She tugged on the zipper of the parka, but it stuck. "Oh, this coat," she muttered, still tugging with one hand while she drove with the other.

"Let me." He reached over, intending only to help her, but his hand brushed against hers, and instant heat exploded in that touch. Flynn's hand jerked upward. He hadn't reacted with such instantaneous attraction to a woman—a woman he'd just met—in a long time. Granted, Samantha Barnett was beautiful, but there was something about her. Something indefinable. A brightness to her smile, to her personality, that seemed to draw him in, make him forget his reporter's objectivity.

Not smart. If there was one thing Flynn prided himself on being, it was smart.

Controlled. He didn't let things get out of hand, get crazy. By keeping tight reins on his life, on himself, he was able to manage everything. The one time he had lost control, he'd nearly lost his career.

He cleared his throat. He clasped the tiny silver zipper and pulled. After a slight catch, the fastener gave way, parting the front of the coat with a low-pitched hum as it slid down.

Beneath the coat, she wore a soft green sweater that dipped in a slight *V* at the neck and skimmed over her curves. From the second he'd met Samantha Barnett, Flynn had noticed the way the green of the sweater enhanced the green in her eyes, offset the golden tones in her hair. But now, without the cover of the apron, he noticed twice as much.

And noticed even more about her.

The scent of her perfume…cinnamon, vanilla, honey—or was it simply the leftover scents of the bakery?—wafted up to tease at his senses. Would her skin taste the same? Taste as good as the baked delights in the cases of the shop?

Flynn drew back. Shook himself.

Get back on track, back in work mode.

Getting distracted by a woman was not part of the plan. It *never* was. He did not get emotionally involved. Did not let himself care, about the people in the story, about people in general. That was how he stayed in control of his life.

No way was he deviating from the road he had laid for himself. Even Mimi, with her need for no real tie, no commitment, fit into what he needed. A woman like Samantha Barnett, who had small-town, commitment values written all over her, would not. "Your, ah, zipper is all fixed."

"Thanks." She flashed that smile his way again.

That was when Flynn MacGregor realized he had a problem. He'd been distracted from the minute he'd walked into that bakery.

Betsy's Bed and Breakfast was located less than six blocks from Earl's repair shop, but with Flynn

MacGregor so close, the ride seemed to take ten hours instead of ten minutes. Sam was aware of his every breath, his every movement. She kept her eyes on the road, not just because visibility had become nearly zero, but because it seemed as if the only thing she saw in her peripheral vision was Flynn.

She hadn't been out on a date in—

Well, a long time. Too much work, too little personal life. That must be why her every thought seemed to revolve around him. Why she'd become hyperaware of the woodsy notes of his cologne. Why her gaze kept straying to his hands, his broad shoulders, the cleft in his jaw.

This ride was a prime opportunity to impress him. To tell him more about the bakery. Not flirt. Not that him jumping in to help with her zipper was flirting…except she had held her breath when he'd gotten so close. Noted the fit of his jacket. The flecks of gold in his eyes. The way the last rays of sun glinted in his hair.

Business, Sam. Business.

"Have you interviewed many bakery owners?" she asked. Then wanted to kick herself. She hadn't exactly hit the witty jackpot with that one.

"A few. Mostly, I cover high-end restaurants. Or, I did." He gave her a wry grin, one that made her wonder about the use of the past tense. "All those chefs courting heart attacks, trying to maintain their five-star ratings."

Sam stopped the Jeep, the four-wheel drive working hard to grip the icy roads, and let a mother and her three children cross the street. Sam recognized Linda Powell, and waved to her through the front window. The littlest Powell waved back, a small red mittened hand bringing a smile to Sam's face. "Is the restaurant business really that competitive?"

He snorted. "Are you kidding? In some cities, these places campaign all year to garner those ratings. They agonize over their menus, stress over the tiniest ingredients, sometimes shipping in a certain fish from one pocket of the world because the chef insists absolutely nothing else will do. Every detail is obsessed over, nitpicked at like it's life and death. They'll accept nothing less than the unqualified best. A bad review can close a place, a good review can skyrocket it to the top."

"But…that's ridiculous." She halted at a stop sign, waiting to make the right onto Maple Street. The Jeep's wipers clicked back and forth, wiping snow off the frosty glass. "A review is simply one person's opinion."

"Ah, but people like me are paid to be the experts." Flynn put a hand on his chest, affecting a dramatic posture. "They live or die by our words."

They had reached Betsy's Bed and Breakfast, where a small hand-painted sign out front announced the converted Victorian's vacancies. Sam stopped in front of the quaint home and parked alongside the front walk. Betsy, a complete Christmas fanatic, had decked the entire porch in holiday flare, with a moving Santa, twinkling lights and even a lighted sleigh and reindeer on the roof.

"And what about me?" Sam asked, turning to Flynn before he exited the Jeep. "What do you think will be my fate? Do you think I'll skyrocket to the top?"

Flynn studied her for a long time, his gaze unreadable in the darkening day, a storm in his blue eyes rivaling the one in the sky. "That, Miss Barnett, is still to be determined."

CHAPTER FOUR

BETSY WILLIAMS, the owner of the bed and breakfast, greeted Flynn with bells on. Literally.

The buxom, wide woman hurried across the foyer and put out her arms, the bells on her house slippers jingling and jangling as she moved, like a one-person reindeer symphony. "Welcome! It's so nice to have another guest! At Betsy's Bed and Breakfast, there's always room for one more!"

Flynn would have turned and run, except Samantha Barnett was standing behind him, blocking the sole exit. "I'm only here until my car is fixed."

And hopefully not a single second longer.

"As long as you want, my heart and home are open to you." She beamed, bright red lips spreading across her face and revealing even, white teeth. Her hand shot out, and she pumped his in greeting, extracting his name and reason for coming to Riverbend in quick succession. "Oh, that's just so exciting!" Betsy said. "Now, tell me what you want for breakfast. Waffles, French toast or eggs?"

Flynn forced a smile to his face. "Surprise me."

Betsy squealed. "I'll delight you, is what I'll do. And I'll have plenty of baked goods to choose from, too, won't I, Sam?"

"You're my first delivery of the day, Betsy. Not to mention, my best customer."

Betsy hustled around and took Flynn's arm, practically hauling him toward the front parlor. "I was her *only* customer, don't you know, back when she first took over. So many people didn't think a girl, still practically a teenager, could run a shop like that. And she did have her mishaps, didn't you, Sam? A few burned things and well, that one teeny-weeny explosion, but you moved past those little setbacks." Betsy beamed. "You're a regular baker now, even if you had no formal training."

Flynn glanced over at Samantha. Her smile seemed held on by strings.

"And those romance cookies, why they worked for me and my Earl. Oh, he's such a cutie, isn't he?" Betsy barreled on, saving Flynn from having to offer an opinion. "Those cookies have fixed up many a person who has come through my door. I serve them every morning on the buffet table." Betsy wagged a finger at him. "If you're looking for love, Mr. MacGregor, you be sure to try those cookies."

"I'm fine, thank you."

She assessed him like a Christmas ham. "I don't see a ring. That means you need the cookies." Betsy nodded. "And our Sam, here, she's available."

"Betsy, Mr. MacGregor needs a room," Sam interjected.

"Oh, my goodness, I almost forgot! And here I am, the hostess and everything." Betsy tsk-tsked herself. "And you need to get back to work, missy, right?"

"I do," Sam replied. "Business is booming lately."

"Well, why wouldn't it? Where else are people going to go to get their cookies? You're the only bakery for miles and miles!" Betsy grinned, as if she'd just paid Samantha a huge compliment. Flynn supposed, in her own way, Betsy thought she had, but he could see the sting in Samantha's eyes. The implication that her success was due solely to a lack of competition, not hard work and expertise. Maybe Betsy still saw Sam as that young kid who burned the muffins.

For a second, his chest constricted with sympathy, then he yanked the emotion back. The first rule in reporting was not to get involved with the story, stay above the fray.

He'd used that as a yardstick to measure every personal decision he'd ever made. After years of sticking to that mantra like tape to a present, Flynn wasn't about to start caring now. To start putting his heart into the mix. He did not cross those boundaries.

Ever.

He didn't care if Riverbend had issues with Sam Barnett or vice versa. Didn't care if her business was going gangbusters or going bust. He'd made a very good living without ever putting his heart into a story, because Flynn MacGregor had learned a long time ago that doing so meant putting his emotions through a meat grinder. He'd rather write about kitchen implements than experience them.

"I'd like to get settled, Miss Williams," Flynn said. "And find out how to log onto your network."

"Network?" She frowned, then propped a fist on her ample hip. "I'll have you know Betsy's Bed and Breakfast is not a chain."

"*Internet* network," Flynn said. "I wanted to check my e-mail."

"Oh, that." She crossed to a side table, to straighten the green-feathered hat on a stuffed cat in an elf costume, then walked back to Flynn. "I don't have one of those either."

"Well, then your dial-up connection. That'll do."

"Dial-up to what? Anytime we need to talk to somebody, we either walk on down to their house or call 'em on the phone." Betsy wagged a finger at him. "By the way, local calls are free at Betsy's Bed and Breakfast, but there is an extra charge for any long distance. The parlor phone is the one set aside for guest usage."

Flynn pivoted back toward Samantha. "There *is* an Internet connection in this town, isn't there?"

"Well, yes, but…" Samantha gave him a smile. "It's not very reliable, so most people here don't bother with it."

He truly had landed in the middle of nowhere. Flynn bit back his impatience, but it surged forward all the same. "What *exactly* does that mean?"

"Meaning when there's a storm, like there is now, the Internet is the first to go."

"What about cable? Satellite?"

"Not here, not yet. Companies look for demand before they start investing the dollars in technology and, well, Riverbend has never been big on embracing that kind of thing." Samantha shrugged.

"How the hell do you do business out here?"

"Most people still do things the old-fashioned way, I suppose. Face-to-face, with a smile and handshake."

A headache began to pound in Flynn's temples. He rubbed at his forehead. He couldn't miss his deadline. Absolutely could not. It wasn't just that *Food Lovers* was holding the Valentine's Day issue especially for this article, and being late would risk raising Tony's ire. Flynn had already earned a slot on the ire list.

There was more than his career to consider. In the last few months since that interview that had blown up in his face, Flynn had found himself searching for—

A connection. To a past he thought he'd shut off, closed like a closet door full of memories no one wanted to look at. He'd done everything he could to take care of that past, to assuage his guilt. But suddenly throwing money at it wasn't enough.

He needed to go in person, even if he wasn't so sure his shoes on that doorstep would be very welcome. Either way, one glance out the window at the storm that had become a frenzy of white, told him the chances of leaving today—even if his car was fixed—were nil.

Until the storm eased, he'd work. Write up this thing about magic elves baking love cookies, or whatever the secret was, turn it over to his editor, and then he could get back to the meat that fed his paycheck and his constant hunger to find the scoop—scathing restaurant reviews exposing the true underbelly of the food industry.

"How am I supposed to work without an Internet connection?" he said.

"We have electricity," Betsy said, her voice high and helpful. "You can plug in a computer. That's good enough, isn't it?" Upstairs, someone called Betsy's name, mentioning an emergency. She sighed. "Oh, Lord, not again." She toodled a wave, then headed up the stairs, while her slippers sang their jarring song.

Flynn turned back to Samantha. "If Scrooge's ghosts do come visit me, they better bring a connection to civilization. And if they can't, just put me out of my misery. Because this place is Jingle Hell."

"He's awful, Aunt Ginny." Sam shuddered. "He hates this town, hates me, I think, and even hates Christmas."

"But he's easy on the eyes. That kind of evens things out, doesn't it?" Ginny Weatherby, who had worked at Joyful Creations for nearly twelve years, smiled at her niece. The two of them were in the back of the bakery, cleaning up and putting it to rights after the busy day. The front half of Joyful Creations was dark, silent, the sign in the window turned to Closed, leaving them in relative peace and quiet. "Your grandmother would have agreed."

"Grandma liked everyone who came through

this door." Sam groaned. "I think he purposely sets out to frustrate me. How am I supposed to give him a good interview? I'm afraid I'll say something I'll regret."

"Oh, you're smart enough not to do that, Sam. I'm sure you'll do fine."

"I don't want him to find out about Grandma," Sam said.

Ginny's gaze softened. "Would it be so bad for people to know?"

Sam toyed with the handle on the sprayer. "I just want people to remember her the way she was, Aunt Ginny."

"They will, Sam." She put a hand on her niece's shoulder. "You need to trust that people of this town are your friends, that they love and care about you, and your grandmother."

"I'll think about it," Sam said. Though she had thought about the same question a hundred times over the past five years, and come back to the same answer. She didn't want people's pity. And most of all, she didn't want them to be hurt when they found out the Joy Barnett they knew and loved was no longer there. "For now, I'm more worried about that Flynn guy. He gets on my last nerve, I swear."

Ginny loaded the dishwasher and pushed a few buttons. "Give him cookies. That'll sweeten him up."

"I did. He wouldn't eat them." Sam sprayed disinfectant on the countertops and wiped them down, using the opportunity to work out some of her frustrations.

Aunt Ginny made a face. "Well, then I don't trust him. Any man who won't eat a plate of cookies, there's something wrong. Unless he's diabetic, then he has an excuse. Did you check for a medical ID bracelet?"

"No. Maybe I should have looked for a jerk bracelet."

"Have some patience, dear." She patted her niece's hand. "This guy could give the shop lots of great publicity."

"I'm trying to be patient."

"And you never know, he could be the one."

Sam rolled her eyes. "Stop trying to fix me up with every man who walks through that door."

Aunt Ginny took off her apron and hung it on a hook by the door, then crossed to her niece. The gentle twinkle of love shone in her light green eyes. "Your mother wouldn't want to see you living your life alone, dear, and neither would your grandmother."

"I'm not alone. I have you."

Sam would forever be grateful to her Aunt Ginny, who had moved to Riverbend from Florida a few months after Sam took over the bakery. Not much of a baker, she hadn't exactly stepped into her sister Joy's shoes, instead becoming the friend and helper Sam needed most. Though making cookies had never been her favorite thing to do, she'd been an enthusiastic supporter of the business, and especially of Sam.

Ginny pursed her lips. "Not the same thing and you know it."

"It's good enough for now. You know why I have to pour everything into the business." Sam went back to wiping, concentrating on creating concentric circles of shine, instead of the thoughts weighing on her. The ones that crept up when she least expected them—reminding her that she had stayed in this shop instead of going to college, getting married, having a family. The part that every so often wondered what if…she didn't have these responsibilities, these expectations?

But she did, so she kept on wiping, and cleaning.

Ginny's hand on her shoulder was a soft reminder that they had visited this topic dozens of times. "You don't have to pour everything into here, dear. Leave some room for you."

"I will," Sam promised, though she didn't mean it. Ginny didn't understand—and never really had—the all-consuming pressure Sam felt to increase business, and revenues. Grandma Joy deserved the best care—and the only way to pay for that was by bringing in more money. Not think about possibilities that couldn't happen.

"And as far as this reporter goes," Ginny said, grabbing her coat as she waited for Sam to finish putting away the cleaning products, "I think it's time you tried the cranberry orange bread. The frosted loaf, not the plain one. I haven't met a person yet that didn't rave about it."

Sam let out a breath, relieved Ginny hadn't suggested sweetening him up with a date, or something else Sam definitely didn't have time or room in her life for. "Okay. I'll bring some over to Betsy's in the morning. Try to sweeten him up."

"And wear your hair up. Put in your hoop earrings, and for God's sake," Aunt Ginny added, wagging a finger, "wear some lipstick."

"Ginny, this isn't a beauty contest, it's an interview."

Ginny grinned. "I didn't get to this age without learning a thing or two about men. And if there's one thing I know, it's to use your assets, Sam," she said, shutting off the lights and closing the shop but not the subject, "every last one."

Flynn woke up in a bad mood.

He flipped open his cell phone, prayed for at least one signal bar, and got none. Moved around the frilly room, over to the lace-curtained window, still nothing. Pushing aside a trio of chubby Santas on the sill, Flynn opened the window, stuck the phone outside as far as his arm would reach and still had zero signal. Where was he? Mars? Soon as he got back to Boston, he was switching wireless carriers. Apparently this one's promise of service "anywhere" didn't include small Indiana towns in the middle of nowhere.

Flynn gave up on his cell phone, got dressed and went downstairs. The scent of freshly brewed coffee drew him like a dog to a bone, pulling him along, straight to the dining room. Several guests sat at one long table, chatting among themselves. Swags of pine ran down the center, punctuated by fat pinecones, puffy stuffed snowmen with goofy grins, unlit red pillar candles. A platoon of Santa plates had been joined by an army of snowman coffee mugs and a cavalry of snowflake-handled silverware. The Christmas invasion had flooded the table, leaving no survivors of ordinary life.

He'd walked into the North Pole. Any minute, he expected dancing elves to serve the muffins.

"Good morning, good morning!" Betsy came jingle-jangling out of the kitchen, her arms wide again. Did the woman have some kind of congenital disease that kept her limbs from hanging at her sides?

"Coffee?" he asked. Pleaded, really.

"On the sideboard. Fresh and hot! Do you want me to get you a cup?"

"I'll help myself. Thanks." He walked over to the poinsettia-ringed carafe, filled a Mrs. Claus mug, then sipped deeply. It took a few minutes for the caffeine to hit his brain.

"I don't know what your travel plans are, but the plows are just now getting to work, and the Indianapolis airport is closed for a couple more hours. They're predicting more snow. I'm so excited. It'll be a white Christmas, for sure!" Betsy applauded the joyful news.

"Thank you for the update." A little snow wouldn't stop him from getting the story out of Samantha Barnett. It might delay his trip down to southern Indiana, but the job—

Nothing delayed the job.

"No problem. It's just one of the many services I provide for my customers. No tip necessary." She beamed. "Oh, and Mr. MacGregor, we'll be singing Christmas carols in the parlor after breakfast, if you'd like to join us."

He'd rather do *anything* but that. "Uh, no. I—"

The front door opened. Flynn turned. Samantha Barnett, her arms loaded with boxes, entered the house. Excellent timing. Flynn hurried forward, taking the top few from her.

"Thanks. I thought I might lose those." She

flashed him a smile that slammed into Flynn with more force than the caffeine's punch.

He told himself it didn't matter, that it hadn't affected him at all. Instead, he put on the friendly face that had won over many an interview subject. "It's not often that I get to come to the rescue of baked goods. Or that they come to mine."

"My goodness, Mr. MacGregor. Did you just make a joke? Because I didn't think you had it in you." Samantha paused in laying the boxes on a small table in the dining room. "Sorry. Sometimes my mouth gets ahead of my brain."

Betsy handed Samantha a set of serving platters, but didn't linger to chat, because one of the guests called her over to ask her a question about local events.

"It's this town," Flynn said after Betsy was gone, keeping his voice low, lest she overhear and come back to argue. "It's like bad lighting on an actress. It brings out the worst in me."

Samantha bristled. "Riverbend? It's not perfect, but I can't imagine why anyone would hate it. You really should give this place a chance before you condemn it. You never know, it might grow on you."

"So do skin rashes."

"You *are* Scrooge," she whispered. "Don't let Betsy hear you say that. People around here are proud of their town."

"I know. She's been trying to recruit me for the caroling crew all morning."

Samantha gave him a nonchalant shrug. "It might do you some good. Infuse you with some Christmas cheer."

Flynn let that subject drop. Infusing wasn't on his menu. He didn't settle in, didn't get to know the locals. Of course, once he came in and ripped apart the local steakhouse in the pages of *Food Lovers*, he wasn't exactly invited back for tea anyway. "You know, there's a big world out there that offers a lot of great things like *civilization*, Internet connections, cellular towers, reliable public transportation. All without paying the price of Christmas carols in the parlor."

Samantha placed the last of the baked goods on the platters and let out a long sigh. "All my life I've dreamed of seeing that world, but…"

"This bakery is as binding as a straightjacket." He'd written that story a hundred times. Shop owners complaining about how small-business life drained them, yet they stayed in the field.

But he understood them. He might not be braising roasts or reducing sauces, but he knew the spirit that drove entrepreneurs. That hunger to climb your own way to the top. To be the only one who fueled success. It didn't matter what it took— long hours, financial worries, constant demands—

to make it from the bottom to the top of the food chain.

Because he had done it himself, and his climb had paid off handsomely. Flynn had become known as the top writer for the food industry and his ambition had created a career that allowed him to call his own shots. Because he was the one that got the story, no matter what it took. No matter how many hours, how many weekends, how many holidays.

He remained unencumbered, without so much as a mortgage, a wife, kids. And though he may have lost his footing this summer—that was a temporary setback. He'd be back on top, after this piece.

"It's not just that the bakery keeps me tied down," Samantha said. "I have other reasons for staying here."

Her tone, almost melancholy, drew him. He could hear the scoop underlying the words, note them like a bloodhound on the trail of a robber. "Like what?"

She quickly pulled herself together. "You're interviewing me about Joyful Creations, Mr. MacGregor, not my personal life." A smile crossed her face, but it was one that had a clear No Trespassing sign. "Let's stick to that, okay?"

"Certainly. Business only, that's the way I like things, too."

Except…she'd intrigued him with the way she'd shut that door so firmly. Most people Flynn interviewed spilled their guts as easily as a two-year-old with an overfilled cup of milk. Samantha Barnett clearly wouldn't be letting a single drop spill.

And he wouldn't let a drop of sympathy spill, either. He refused to fall for whatever had brought that wisp of emotion to her eyes. To let her move past his reporter curiosity.

Except…a part of him did wonder about the story behind the story. He had to be crazy. Clearly made delusional by all this Christmas spirit surrounding him. That was it.

Except, Flynn wasn't a Christmas spirit kind of guy.

"How's the weather out there?" Flynn asked, even though he already knew the answer. His comment was simply meant to retreat to neutral ground. He'd circle around to the article in a while, once he got his head back in the game.

"The storm has eased a bit, but they're expecting another front to move in, later this morning."

"If Earl's got the part for my car, that gives me just enough time to get out of town, if you have time for us to finish our interview before I have to go."

Samantha laughed. "Go and do what? The road travel will be awful again in a couple of hours, not that it's all that great right now to begin with. You might as well stay. In fact, I don't think you'll have a choice."

"There's always a choice, Miss Barnett."

"Well, unless you convince the National Guard to convoy you out, Mr. MacGregor, I think your only choice is to stay put." She closed the last of the boxes and stacked them into a pile. "I have to get back to the shop, but if you want to finish your interview, I'll be free at lunch for twenty minutes or so."

He'd be here all day, from the sounds of it. Have hours and hours of time to kill. He could, most likely, get what he needed from Samantha Barnett in twenty minutes. But the idea of rushing the questions, scribbling down the answers over a corned beef on rye—

Simply didn't appeal like it normally did. He must be in need of a vacation. Why else would he not be in a rush to meet his deadline? To move on to the next headline?

"No," he said.

"No?" One eyebrow perked up.

"I want more than that."

"More?" Now the other eyebrow arched.

"Dinner." The noise from the other bed-and-breakfast guests had risen, so Flynn took a step closer, and caught the scent of vanilla in her hair. Had he just said that word? Offered a dinner date?

Yes, he had, and now, he found himself

lowering his voice, not for intimacy he told himself, but for privacy. Yet, everything about their closeness, the words, spelled otherwise. "A long, lingering dinner. No rushing out to fill boxes with cranberry muffins or to bring frosted reindeer to screaming three-year-olds."

"Just you and me…"

"And my pen and notepad. This is an interview, not a date, Miss Barnett," Flynn added, clarifying as much for himself as for her.

"Of course." Her gaze lingered on his, direct and clear. "But either way, would you do me one favor?"

"What?"

"Stop calling me Miss Barnett. I feel like a schoolteacher, or worse, the lone spinster in town, when you do that. My name is Samantha, but my friends call me Sam. Let's start with that."

He nodded. "Sam it is." Her name slipped off his tongue as easily as a whisper.

"And one more thing." She picked up a cookie from one of the platters and held it out to him. "I'm not leaving here until I know you've tasted my wares."

His grin quirked up on one side. "That could be taken in many ways, Sam."

She brought the cookie to his lips. "The only way I'm meaning is the white chocolate chip kind, Mr. MacGregor."

"Call me Flynn, and I'll do whatever you ask."
Was he *flirting*? He never did that. Ever. Maybe
Betsy had spiked the coffee.

"Flynn," she said, so softly, he was sure he'd
never heard his name spoken like that before,
"please take a bite."

"These aren't those special romance cookies,
are they?"

"No," Sam said. "Although my Great-Aunt
Ginny thinks I should give one to every eligible
male that crosses my path."

Her face colored, and he knew she regretted
sharing that tidbit. So. Samantha Barnett's life
was a bit lonelier than she wanted to admit.

"You've never tried them?" he asked. Then
wondered why he cared.

"No. But I assure you, Flynn, that my white
chocolate macadamia nut cookies are just as delicious." A smile crossed her lips. "And even
better, there's absolutely no danger of falling in
love if you eat one."

Before he could tell himself that it was far
smarter to resist, to ignore whatever silly, impractical feelings Sam had awakened in him,
Flynn found his lips parting and his mouth accepting the sweet morsel.

The minute the cookie hit his palate, Flynn
knew this interview would be unlike any other.

And that would be a problem indeed.

CHAPTER FIVE

SAM CHANGED into a dress. Out of a dress. Into jeans. Out of jeans. Into a skirt. Out of the skirt and back into the jeans. Finally, she settled on a deep green sweater with pearl beading around the collar and black slacks, with pointy-toed dress boots. Nothing too sexy, or that screamed trying to impress the guy.

Even if she was.

Though she couldn't say why. Flynn MacGregor had been incredibly disagreeable, and not at all her kind of man. Even if he did have nice hands. Deep blue eyes. Broad shoulders. And a way of entering a room that commanded attention.

All that changing and fussing over her appearance made her ten minutes late. She entered Hall's Steaks and Ribs, brushing the snow from her hair and shoulders, half expecting Flynn to make a note in his notebook about the Joyful

Creations' owner's lack of punctuality. Instead, he simply gave her a nod, not so much as a smile, and rose to pull out her chair. "Is it still snowing?"

Okay, so she was a little disappointed that he hadn't said she looked pretty. Hadn't acknowledged her one iota as a woman.

She was here for an interview, not a date. To grow her business. "It's a light snow now. The weatherman said we'll only get another inch or two tonight."

"Good. Hopefully Earl has my car fixed and I can get back on the road in the morning." Flynn took the opposite seat, then handed one of the menus to Sam.

She put it to the side. "Thank you. But I already know what I want."

"Eat here often?"

"When there's only one restaurant in town, this is pretty much *the* date hot spot." Sam felt her face heat. Why had she mentioned dates?

"Are you here often? On dates?" He glanced around the dark cranberry-and-gold room, decorated in a passably good imitation of Italianate style, considering the building was a modern A-frame. The restaurant was crowded, the hum of conversation providing a steady buzz beneath the instrumental Christmas carols playing on the sound system.

"Me?" Sam laughed. "Yeah, in all my spare time. Like those five minutes I had back in 2005."

He let out a chuff. "Probably the same five I had."

A waitress came by their table—a willowy blonde on the Riverbend High School pep squad whose name temporarily eluded Sam's memory—and dropped off two glasses of water, but didn't pause long enough to take their orders.

"You must travel a lot for your job," Sam said.

Flynn took a sip and nodded. "About half the year I'm on the road. The other half I'm behind a computer."

"So I'm not the only workaholic in the room?"

"My job demands long hours."

Sam arched a brow. "Oh, I get it. You're a special case. Whereas I'm…" She trailed off, leaving him to fill in the blank.

"Ambitious, too." He tipped his glass toward her, in a touché gesture.

"Exactly. Then you can understand why I want to expand the shop."

"I do. I just think you should understand what you're getting yourself into when you start pursuing fame, fortune, the American dream."

"I do." The way he'd said the words, though, made Sam feel as if what she wanted was wrong. That she was being self-serving. Had she expressed her dream wrong? No, she hadn't. He'd simply misinterpreted her.

Besides, Flynn MacGregor didn't know the whole story, nor did he need to. She *had* to get out of Riverbend. Away, not just from this town, but from things she couldn't change, things she'd given up on a long time ago. The life she'd wished she could have had, and had put on hold for so long, it had slipped through her fingers. Maybe then—

Maybe then she'd find peace.

Flynn picked up his menu and studied the two pages of offerings. "And where do you fit into that equation?"

"What's that supposed to mean?"

"Exactly what I said." His voice was slightly muffled by the vinyl-bound menu.

"You mean, free time for me?"

Flynn put the menu down. "From what I've heard around town, you're not exactly…the social butterfly. You work. And you work. And you *work*. You're like a squirrel providing for a never-ending winter."

"You write for this industry. Of everyone, you should know how demanding a bakery can be."

"That's what the classified ads are for. To hire people to bake."

"People around here," Sam began, then lowered her voice, realizing how many of those very people were situated right beside her, "expect the baked goods to be made by a family member. Third generation, and all that."

He scoffed. "Oh come on. In this age of automation, you don't actually think that everyone believes you're truly popping on every last gumdrop button?"

She stared at him, as if he was insane. "But I do."

"Who is going to know if you do it, or a monkey from the zoo does?" Flynn asked.

"Well…I will, for one."

"And the harm in that is…?" He put out his hands. "You might actually have some free time to see a movie? Go out on a date? Have a life?"

She shifted in her chair. His words sprung like tiny darts, hitting at the very issues Sam did her best to avoid. "I have a life."

Flynn arched a brow. "You want me to write the story for you? Young, ambitious restaurateur, or in your case—" he waved a hand in her direction "—baker, goes into the business thinking she'll be *different*." He put special emphasis on the last word, tainting it with disgust.

"My circumstances were different."

But Flynn went on, as if he hadn't even heard her. "She thinks she'll find a way to balance having an outside life with work. That she'll be the one to learn from her peers, to balance the business with reality. That she, and only she, can find the secret to rocketing to the top while still holding on to some semblance of normality." He leaned forward, crossing his arms on the table. "Am I close?"

"No." The lie whistled through her lips.

"Listen, I admire your dedication, I really do. But let me save you the peek at the ending. You won't end up any different than anyone else. You'll look back five, ten, twenty years from now, and think 'where the hell did my life go?'"

"Who made you judge and jury over me?" Sam's grip curled around her water glass, the temptation to throw the beverage in his face growing by the second. "I'm doing what I have to do."

"Do you?"

"What?"

"Have to?"

His piercing gaze seemed to ask the very questions she never did. The ones that plagued her late at night when she was alone in the house her grandmother used to own, pacing the floors, wondering…

What if.

Before she had to come up with an answer, the waitress returned, introduced herself as Holli with an i and took out a notepad. "What can I get you?"

"Lasagna with extra sauce on the side," Sam said, grateful for the change in subject.

"I'll have the same." Flynn handed his menu to Holli, who gave each of them a perky smile before heading to the kitchen. "Enough of me giving you the ugly truth about your future. I'm not here to play psychic."

"And I'm not asking for your advice."

"True." A grin quirked up one side of his mouth. "I get the feeling you're not the kind of person who would take my advice, even if I gave it."

His smile was contagious, and she found herself answering with one of her own. He had charm, she had to give him that. Grudgingly. "I might. Depending on what you had to say."

"Admit it. You're stubborn."

"I am not." She paused. "Too stubborn."

He laughed then, surprising her, and by the look on his face, probably even himself. "Now there's a line I should quote." He dug out his pen and paper.

Disappointment curdled in Sam's stomach. "Are you always after the story?"

He glanced up. "That's my job."

"Yeah, but…just like you were saying to me, don't you ever take a moment for you?"

His blue gaze met hers, direct and powerful. "You mean treat this as a date, instead of an interview?"

"Well—" Sam shifted again "—not *that* exactly."

The grin returned, wider this time. "How long *has* it been?"

"Has it been for what?"

"Since you've been out on a date?"

Sam took such a deep sip of water, she nearly drowned. "I could ask you the same thing."

"My answer's easy. A week."

"Oh." She put the glass down. "I thought you said you didn't have that much free time."

"I was exaggerating. I'm a writer." That grin again. "Given to hyperbole and all that."

Was he…flirting with her? Holy cow. Was that why everything within her seemed touched with fever? Why her gut couldn't stop flip-flopping? Why she alternately wanted to run—and to stay?

It was simply because he was right. She hadn't been out on a date in forever. She wasn't used to this kind of head-on attention from a man. Especially a man as good at the head-on thing as he was.

"So which would you rather?" Flynn asked. "A date? Or an interview?"

The interview, her mind urged. Say interview. The business. The bakery needed the increase in revenue. Her personal life could wait, just as it always had. The business came first.

"A date."

Had she really just said that? Out loud? To the man who held the future of Joyful Creations in his pen? Sam's face heated, and her feet scrambled back, ready to make a fast exit.

But instead of making a note on his ubiquitous notepad, Flynn leaned back in his chair and smiled. "You surprise me, Samantha Barnett. Just when I think you're all work and no fun, you opt for a little fun."

"Maybe I'm not the cardboard character you think."

"Maybe you're not." His voice had dropped into a range that tickled at her gut, sent her thoughts down a whole other path that drifted away from fun and into man-and-woman-alone territory. He pushed the notepad to the side, then leaned forward, his gaze connecting with hers. When he did that, it seemed as if the entire room, heck, the entire world, dropped away. "Well, if this *was* a date, and we were back in Boston, instead of the pits of Christmastown here, do you want to know what we'd be doing?"

"Yes," Sam replied, curiosity pricking at her like a pin. "Why not?"

He thought a second, considering her. "Well, since you haven't been out on a date in a while, our first date should be something extraordinary."

"Extraordinary?" she echoed.

"A limo, for starters. Door-to-door service."

"A limo?" She arched a brow. "On a reporter's salary?"

"I've done very well in my field. And they tend to reward that handsomely."

Quite handsomely if the expensive suit, cashmere coat and Italian leather shoes were any indication. "What next, after the limo?"

"Dinner, maybe at Top of the Hub, a restaurant at the top of the Prudential building in Boston. Lobster, perhaps? With champagne, of course."

"Of course," she said, grinning, caught in the web of the fantasy, already imagining herself whisked away in the long black car, up the elevator to the restaurant, sipping the golden bubbly drink. "And after dinner?"

"Dancing. At this little jazz club I know where the lights are dimmed, music is low and sexy and there's only enough room for me to hold you close. Very, very close."

Sam swallowed. Her heart raced, the sound thundering in her head. "That sounds like quite the place."

"A world away from this one."

A world away. The world she had dreamed of once, back when she'd thought she was going to college, going places—

Going somewhere other than Riverbend and the bakery.

For just a second, Sam allowed her mind to

wander, to picture a different future. One without the bakery to worry about, without the future of several potential additional locations to fret over. Without other people to worry about, to care for.

What if she were free of all that and could pursue a love life, a marriage, a family? A man who looked at her with desire like Flynn did—

And she had time to react, to date him? To live her life like other women did?

Guilt smacked her hard. She didn't have time to dally with those thoughts. Too many people were depending on her. Later, Sam reminded herself with an inward sigh.

Later, it would be her turn.

Sam looked away, breaking eye contact with Flynn MacGregor. With the temptation he offered, as easily as a coin in his palm. She toyed with her silverware, willing her heart to slow, her breath to return to normal, and most of all, her head to come down from the clouds. "Well, that would be nice. If I lived somewhere else besides here."

"If you did. Which you don't." Flynn cleared his throat, as if he, too, wanted to get back to business, to put some distance between them. "So, tell me. Why the lasagna?"

Of all the questions he could have asked, that one had to be the last one Sam would have expected. "I like lasagna, and the way they make it here is even better than my grandmother did—does," she corrected herself. Darn. She had to be more careful. Sam brushed her hair off her face and opted for another topic, trying to stay on safe, middle ground. "Don't you meet many women who like lasagna?"

That made him laugh. Flynn MacGregor's laugh was deep and rich, like good chocolate. "No. Definitely not. Most of the women I know spend their entire day obsessing about how to whittle their waists down to the next single digit."

Sam patted her hips. "Well, as you can see, that's definitely not me. My waist has never been considered whittled. Though maybe if I did cut back on the—"

"Don't." Flynn's steady gaze met hers. "Enjoy the lasagna. Your waist is perfect just the way it is."

Heat pooled in Sam's gut. Other men had looked at her with desire of course. She'd had boyfriends who had made her feel wanted, even pretty, but never before had a single sentence set off a blast of fireworks in her veins. And here was this big-city playboy, seeing her as a sexy woman.

"You don't have to butter me up," she said. "I already agreed to the interview."

He leaned forward in his seat, his blue eyes assessing her intently. "I'm not buttering you up for anything at all. You look beautiful tonight, Sam."

A trill of joy ran through Sam, skating down her spine. "Well then, thank you." She felt a blush fill her face, and she cursed under her breath. Time to get the focus off herself. Every time he looked at her like that, she got distracted from what was important. "I've told you plenty about me. It's your turn."

He paused. "I'm from Boston. I write for a magazine. I live alone, have no pets."

She laughed. "You're not a man who shares a lot about himself, are you?"

"Just the facts, ma'am." He smiled.

But behind that smile, an invisible wall had been erected. Curiosity rose in Sam. What made Flynn MacGregor tick? What made him smile? Until tonight, he'd rarely done so. When his mouth did curve into a grin, the gesture transformed his face, his eyes, and seemed to make him into an entirely different person. The kind of person she would—under other circumstances— want to get to know.

Not today. Despite their agreement to put the interview on hold, she reminded herself to watch her words. Aunt Ginny's warning about *Food Lovers'* tendency to want the story behind the story came back to Sam. She'd have to be on guard tonight. Flynn MacGregor could be doing all this simply to get her to open up.

And not because he wanted her.

She should be happy. For one, she had no time for a relationship. She had a business to run, a business that was on the cusp of taking off and becoming something so much bigger than this little town, that corner location. She had people depending on her to take Joyful Creations to the next level—and getting sidetracked by dating was just not part of the recipe.

But what if it could be?

The lasagna arrived, and Flynn immediately took a bite of the steaming Italian food. "It pays to follow the locals when ordering food. This is delicious."

"I know. It may say steaks and ribs on the sign out front, but the owner is a full-blooded Italian, so that's his specialty, which also explains the décor. I think he just has the other things on the menu, because that's what tourists expect when they come to Indiana. Not that we get many in Riverbend, at least until the last few weeks."

"Because of the airline magazine's mention of the shop."

Sam buttered two pieces of bread, and handed one slice to Flynn, who thanked her. "That article, and the boost in business, was a blessing and a half, but one that has kept us hopping from sunup to sundown. In fact, after I leave here, I'm going back to the shop to get a start on tomorrow's baking."

"Tonight? But you already put in a long day, didn't you?"

"That's the life of a baker. No free time."

"And yet, you want more."

"I'm not a sugar addict, Flynn. I'm a success addict." She shot him a smile.

Flynn pulled his notepad over and jotted down those words. If anything reminded her this wasn't a date, that did. A flicker of disappointment ran through her, but Sam brushed it off.

For a minute, he'd given her the gift of a normal life. Let her feel again like a normal woman, a beautiful woman. That would be enough. For a while.

A really long while.

"Why?" he asked.

"Why does anyone want success?" Sam bent her head and took a bite of food, chewed and swallowed. "To prove you did well with your business."

"That's all? No other reason?"

No other reason she wanted in print. "That's all." She signaled to Holli to box up her dinner and pushed her plate to the side, her appetite gone. But that wasn't what had her wanting to get out of the restaurant so bad. It was the way Flynn kept studying her, as if he could see behind every answer she'd given him, as if he knew she was holding something back. "Is that all you need? Because I really have to get back to the shop."

"Sure. Thank you for your time, Miss—" He paused. "Sam."

She reached into her purse to pull out some money for dinner but Flynn stopped her with a touch of his hand on hers. A surge of electricity ran up her arm.

"My treat," he said.

"I thought you said this wasn't a date."

"It's not. I have an expense account."

Once again, disappointment whistled through her as brisk and fast as winter's winds. "Oh. Well, in that case, thank you." Sam rose and grabbed her coat off the back of her chair. "If you have any other questions, call me at the shop. That's pretty much where I live." She turned to go.

"Wait."

Sam pivoted back, part of her still hoping— some insane part—that all this really had been a date, and not an interview. "Yes?"

"You mentioned something about having dial-up Internet access at Joyful Creations. Do you think I could come by tonight, if you're going to be there anyway, and access my e-mail?" A grin flashed on Flynn's face. "I'm having acute with-drawal symptoms. Fever, aches, pains, the whole nine yards."

She'd been wrong.

He wanted her—but for her Internet connection only. That was for the best. Even if it didn't feel that way.

"Certainly," Sam said. "Like I said, that shop is my life."

CHAPTER SIX

FLYNN STARED at the picture for a long time. The edges had yellowed, the image cracked over the years, but the memories were as fresh as yesterday. Two boys smiling, their hair tousled by the wind whisking up the Atlantic and onto Savin Hill Beach, their grins as wide as the Frisbees they held in their hands. One day, out of thousands, but that one day—

Had been a good one.

Flynn put the picture back in his wallet, flipped open his cell phone and scrolled through his contact list until he got to the name Liam.

Flynn shut the phone without dialing. He didn't have a signal anyway. Not that he would have called if he had. He hadn't dialed that number in over a year.

Liam hadn't answered his calls in two.

He'd driven all this way, with a crazy idea that maybe Liam would see him if Flynn called. If he said he was a few towns away, and asked if Liam wanted to see him? Or maybe if he just showed up on Liam's doorstep and surprised him, saying "hey, it's Christmas, why don't we just put all this behind us?"

Flynn shook his head. Maybe too much time had passed to heal old wounds.

Flynn rose and put his wallet into his back pocket. He swallowed back the memories, the whiff of nostalgia—had it been nostalgia or something else?—that had hit him for a brief second, then grabbed his laptop and headed out of the bed and breakfast and over to Sam's shop.

From outside the window, he could see her inside, softly lit by a single overhead light, the golden glow spreading over her features. If he hadn't known better, he'd have thought she was an image from a Christmas card—the painted kind famous for their lighting and muted colors.

Flynn shook off the thought. What was with him today? He was going soft, that was for sure. First, the picture, followed by the quick detour down Memory Lane, then the temptation to call Liam, and finally the comparison of this woman to an artist's impression, for Pete's sake. He was not the emotional type. Clearly, he needed to get out of this odd little town and back to the city. He entered the shop, his presence announced by a set of jingle bells above the entrance.

Jingle bells. He scoffed. Of course.

"I'm in the kitchen," Sam called to him.

He headed through the darkened shop, pulled as much by her voice as by the scent of baked goods. The quiet notes of vanilla, mixed with the more pungent song of nutmeg, all muted by the melody of fruits and nuts. The scents triggered a memory but it was gone before he could grasp it. "Smells good in here."

She looked up and brushed a tendril of blond hair off her forehead with the back of her hand. "Thanks. I'm usually too busy to notice anything other than how low the flour supply is getting."

He slipped onto a stainless steel stool in the corner and laid his laptop on the small desk beside him. "Don't you take breaks to taste the cookies? Dip into the muffins?"

"Me? No. I rarely have time."

"Didn't we already have this discussion about all work and no play…?" He let the old axiom trail off, tossing her a grin.

She gestured toward his computer. "Hey, speak for yourself, Mr. Nose to the Grindstone."

Right. Get back to work. Flynn had no intentions of missing this deadline, because doing so meant putting his road trip on hold, and even though he wasn't so sure of the reception he'd receive, he knew it was time to see Liam. That meant he needed to check in with the office and get a head start on writing his article. Procrastinating wasn't going to restore his reputation at the magazine, nor was it going to get him any closer to seeing Liam. "Speaking of which… Can I use your Internet connection?"

"If you get lucky." Sam colored. "I, ah, didn't mean that the way it came out. I meant—"

"If the lines are working."

"Yes." She nearly breathed her relief.

"I wouldn't have thought anything else."

But hadn't he, for just a second? Samantha Barnett was an attractive woman. Curvaceous, friendly and she was surrounded by the perfume of cookies. Any man with a pulse would be enticed by her, as he had been—very much so— at dinner a little while ago. Mimi had never seemed so far away.

Not that he and Mimi had what anyone would really call a relationship. They were more…convenience daters. When either of them needed someone to attend a function or to see a movie with, they picked up the phone. Days could go by before they talked to each other, the strings as loose as untied shoelaces. Mimi liked it that way, and so did Flynn.

Samantha Barnett, who wore her small-town roots like a coat, was definitely not a convenience dater. He'd do best to keep his heart out of that particular cookie jar.

Flynn cleared his throat, turned to his bag and unpacked his laptop, plugging the machine into the outlet on the wall and the telephone line into his modem. Sam gave him a phone number to dial and connect to her provider. He typed in all the information, then waited for the magic to happen.

Nothing. No familiar musical tones of dialing. No screeching of the modem. No hiss of a telephone line. Just an error message.

He tried again. A third time. Powered down the computer, powered it back up and tried connecting a fourth time.

"No luck?" Sam asked.

"Are you sure we're not on Mars?"

Sam laughed. "Pretty sure. Though there are days…" She tossed him a smile, while her hands kept busy dropping balls of chocolate chip cookie dough onto a baking sheet. "That remoteness, that disconnect from city life, is all part of the charm of Riverbend, though. And what draws those droves of tourists."

Flynn shot her a look of disdain. "All five of them? Not counting your temporary flood, of course."

"Actually, it's pretty busy here in the summer. And you saw the lines outside the shop today. People from big cities really like the rural location, and the fact that we have lots of lakes nearby for boating and camping."

"The cityfolk roughing it, huh?"

"Yep. Except we have running water here." Again, another grin. He noticed that when she smiled, her green eyes sparkled with gold flecks. They were the color of the forest just after a storm, when the sun was beginning to peek through the clouds.

Or maybe that was just the reflection from the overhead lights. Yeah, that was it.

Flynn gave up on his computer and shut the laptop's cover. He rose and crossed to Sam. Was it the light? Or was it her eyes? "Why do you live here?"

She paused in making cookies, as if surprised by the question. The scent of vanilla wafted up from the dough. "I grew up here."

He took another step closer. Only because he still couldn't decide what caused the gold flecks in her eyes. Mother Nature or sixty watts. He'd been intrigued all night, first in the restaurant and now, wondering, pondering… thinking almost nonstop about her. A bad sign in too many ways to count, but he told himself if he could just solve this mystery of her eyes, the thoughts would stop. "Okay, then why did you stay? You didn't have to keep the business open. You could have closed it and moved on."

She opened her mouth, then shut it again, as if

she had never considered this question before. "Joyful Creations has been in my family for three generations. My family was depending on me to keep it open."

Another step. Flynn inhaled, and he swore he could almost taste the air around Sam. It tasted like...

Sugar cookies.

"What did you say?" Sam said.

Had he said that out loud? Damn. What the hell was wrong with him? He did *not* get emotionally involved with his interview subjects.

He did *not* lose his focus.

He did *not* forget the story. He went after it, whatever the cost.

Flynn backed up three steps, returned to his laptop and flipped up the top. It took a few seconds for the hibernating screen to come back to life. Several long, agonizing seconds of silence that Flynn didn't bother to fill. "If it's all the same to you, I'd like to work here for a little while. That way, if I have any questions while I'm writing, I can just ask them." Meaning, he intended to probe deeper into the clues she'd dropped at dinner, but he didn't say that. "And, I can try to connect to the Internet again."

"Sure." Her voice had a slight, confused lilt at the end. She put the sheet of cookies into the oven, then started filling another one.

Keeping his back to her, Flynn sought the familiarity of his word processing program. He tugged his notepad out of his bag and began typing. The words did what they always did— provided a cold, objective distance. It was as if the bright white of the screen and the stark blackness of the letters erased all emotion, scrubbed away any sense of Flynn's personality. He became an outside observer, reporting facts.

And nothing else.

He wrote for ten minutes, his fingers moving so fast, the words swam before his eyes. Usually, when he wrote a story, pulling the paragraphs out of his brain was like using camels to drag a mule through the mud. He'd never been a fast writer, more a deliberate one.

But this time, it seemed as if his brain couldn't keep up with his hands. He wrote until his fingers began to hurt from the furious movement across the keyboard. When he sat back and looked at the page count, he was stunned to see he had five solid pages in the file already.

Flynn scrolled up to the opening paragraph, expecting his usual "Established in blah-blah year, this business" opening, followed by the punch of personal information, the tabloid zing he was known for. Nearly all his stories had that straightforward, get-to-the-facts approach that led to the one nugget everyone else had missed. It was what his editor liked about him. He delivered the information, with a minimal peppering of adjectives.

"Can I read it?" Sam asked.

He hadn't even realized she had moved up behind him. But now he was aware, very aware. He jerked back to the real world, to the scent of fresh-baked cookies, and to Samantha Barnett, standing right behind him.

"Uh, sure. Keep in mind it's a first draft," he said. "And it's just the facts, none of the fluff kind of thing the airline magazine…" His voice trailed off as his eyes connected with the first few paragraphs on the screen.

"Visions of sugar plums dance in the air. The sweet perfume of chocolate hangs like a cloud. And standing amidst the magic of this Christmas joy, like the star atop a tree, is the owner of Joyful Creations, Samantha Barnett.

"She knows every customer by name, and has a smile for everyone who walks through the door of her shop, no matter how many muffins she's baked or how many cookies she's boxed that day. She's as sweet as the treats in her cases…."

Flynn slammed the top of the laptop shut. What the *hell* was that?

"Wow." A slow smile spread across Sam's face. "And here I thought you were going to write one of those scathing exposés, the kind I've heard the magazine is famous for. I mean, you barely tasted any of the food here and…"

"And what?" he asked, scowling. He did *not* write that kind of drivel. He was known as a bulldog, the writer that went for the jugular, got the story at all costs. Not this sweet-penning novelist wanna-be.

"And well…it didn't seem like you liked me."

He didn't know how to answer that. *Did* he like her? And what did it matter if he did or didn't? He'd be leaving this town the second his car was fixed and the roads were clear. After that, Samantha Barnett would simply be one more file among the dozens in his cabinet. "I don't like this town. It's a little too remote for me." That didn't answer the question of whether he liked her, he realized.

Either way, his editor was expecting a Flynn MacGregor story. The kind free of emotion, but steeped in details no other publication had been able to find. Flynn dug and discovered, doing whatever it took to get the real story. That chase was what had thrilled him from his first days as a cub reporter at a newspaper, and it was what had made him a legend at the magazine.

Getting the story was a game—a game he played damn well.

Sam crossed her arms over her chest and stared at him. "Ever since you arrived here, I've been trying to figure you out. Aunt Ginny would tell me that if I had any common sense at all, I'd keep my mouth shut, but I've never been very good at that."

He had turned toward her, and when they'd both been reading the story on his computer, the distance between them had closed. Now Flynn found himself watching that mouth. A sassy mouth, indeed. "And I suppose you're about to tell me exactly what you think of me? Point out all my faults?"

"You do have a few." She inhaled, and the *V* of her sweater peeked open just enough to peak his desire.

She had more than a sassy mouth, that was for sure. He reached out and tipped her chin upward. "What if I do the same for you?"

She swallowed, but held his gaze. Desire burned in his veins, pounding an insistent call in his brain. Everything within him wanted to kiss her, take her in his arms, end this torturous curiosity about what she'd feel like. Taste like.

And yet, at the same time, the reporter side of him tried to shush that desire, told him to take advantage of the moment, to use it to exploit the vulnerable moment.

"I'm not the one going around with a chip the size of Ohio on my shoulder," she said.

"Maybe I have a good reason for that chip."

"At Christmas? No one has a good reason to be grumpy at Christmas."

He released her jaw. "Some people do."

The clock above them ticked, one second, two. Three. Then Sam's voice, as quiet as snow falling. "Why?"

The clock got in another four ticks before Flynn answered. "Let's just say I never stayed in one place long enough for Santa to find me."

"Why?"

A one-word question. One that, in normal conversation, might have prompted a heartfelt discussion. Some big sharing moment over a couple cups of coffee and a slice of streusel. But Flynn wasn't a coffee-and-streusel kind of guy. He hadn't done show-and-tell in first grade, and he wasn't going to do it now.

The oven timer buzzed, announcing another batch of cookies was done. And so was this conversation. Somehow it had gotten turned around, and Flynn was off his game, off his center of gravity. He needed to retreat and regroup.

"The story is about you, not me," Flynn said. "When you get a job as a reporter, then you get to ask the questions."

Without bothering to pack it in the bag, he picked up his laptop, yanked the cord out of the outlet and headed out of the warm and cozy shop.

And into a biting cold, the kind he knew as well as his own name.

This was the world where Flynn found comfort, not the one he'd just left.

Today her grandmother thought she was the maid.

Sam told herself not to be disappointed. Every time she drove over to Heritage Nursing Home, she steeled herself for that light of confusion in Joy Barnett's eyes, that "Do I know you?" greeting instead of the hugs and love Sam craved like oxygen.

And every time disappointment hit her like a snowplow.

"Have you cleaned the bathroom?" Joy asked. "I'm afraid I made a mess of the sink when I washed my face. I'm sorry."

Sam worked up a smile. "Yes, I cleaned it."

It took all Sam had not to release the sigh in her throat. How she wanted things to change, to turn back the clock. There used to be days when her grandmother had recognized her, before the Alzheimer's had robbed her grandmother of the very joy that she had been named for. The smiles of recognition, the friendships, the family members, and most of all the memories. It was as if she'd become a disconnected boat, floating alone in a vast ocean with no recognizable land, no horizon.

So Sam had, with reluctance, finally put Grandma Joy into Heritage Nursing Home. The care there was good, but Sam had visited another, much more expensive facility several miles away from Riverbend. The bakery simply didn't make enough money, at least with a single location, to pay for Grandma Joy's care at the other facility, one that boasted a special Alzheimer's treatment center with a nostalgic setting, an aromatherapy program and several hands-on patient involvement programs designed to help stimulate memory and brain activity. It might not bring her grandmother back to who she used to be, but Sam hoped the other facility would give her grandmother a better quality of life than Heritage Nursing Home, which was nice, but offered none of those specialized care options.

After all Grandma Joy had done for Sam, from taking her in as a child to raising her with the kind of love that could only be called a gift, Sam would do anything to make the rest of Joy's years happy, stress-free and as wonderful as possible. There might not be any way to bring back the grandmother she remembered, but if this other center could help ease the fearful world of unfamiliarity that Joy endured, then Sam would sacrifice anything to bring that to the woman she considered almost a mother.

Including living her own life. For a while longer.

Grandma Joy looked at Sam expectantly, as if she thought Sam might whip out a broom and start sweeping the floor. Sam held out a box. "Here, I brought you something."

Joy took the white container and beamed. "Oh, aren't you sweet." She flipped open the lid and peeked inside. "How did you know these were my favorite?"

Sam's smile faltered. Her throat burned. "Your granddaughter told me."

Grandma Joy looked up, a coconut macaroon in her hand. "My granddaughter? I have a granddaughter?"

Sam nodded. Tears blurred her vision. "Her name is Samantha."

Joy repeated the name softly, then thought for a moment. "Samantha, of course. But Sam's just a baby. She can't hardly talk, so she can't tell you about my favorite cookies, silly. She is the cutest thing, though. Everyone who meets her just loves her. She comes to the bakery with me every day." She leaned forward. "Did I tell you I own a bakery?"

"Yes, you did."

"My husband and I started it when we first got married. So much work, but oh, we've had a lot of fun. Sam loves being there, she really does. She's my little helper. Someday, Sam and I are going to run it together." Joy sat back in the rose-patterned armchair. As her thoughts drifted, her gaze drifted out the window, to the snow-covered grounds. The white flakes glistened like crystals, hung in long strings of diamonds from the trees. She sighed. "That will be a wonderful day."

"Yes," Sam said, closing her eyes, because it was too painful to look at the same view as her grandmother, "it will."

Sam Barnett was leaving something out of her personal recipe. Flynn had rewritten the article into one more closely resembling the kind he normally wrote—where that poetic thing had come from last night, he had no idea—and realized not all the whys had been answered. There was still something, he wasn't sure what, that he needed to know. But the bulldog in him knew he'd yet to find that missing piece.

He had to dig deeper. Keep pawing at her, until he got her to expose those personal bits that would give his article the meat it needed. The kind of tidbits *Food Lovers'* readers ate like candy.

It was, after all, what he was known for. What would put him right back on top. Then why had he hesitated? Normally, he did his interviews, in and out in a day, two at most. He never lingered. Never let a subject rattle him like she had last night.

Damn it, get a hold of yourself. Get the story, and get out of town.

Flynn rose, stretching the kinks out of his back he'd picked up from sitting in the uncomfortable wooden chair at the tiny desk in his room. He crossed to the window and parted the lacy curtains. Outside, snow had started to fall.

Again.

Where the hell was he? Nome, Alaska? For Pete's sake, all it did was snow here.

He pulled on his coat, and hurried downstairs. Betsy, who was sitting behind the piano in the front parlor, tried to talk him into joining the out-of-tune sing-along with the other guests, but Flynn waved a goodbye and headed out of the bed and breakfast, turning up his collar against the blast of cold and ice. By the time he made it to Earl's garage, his shoes and socks were soaked through, and his toes had become ten Popsicles.

"Well, howdy-ho," Earl said when Flynn entered the concrete-and-brick structure. He had on his plaid earflap hat and a thick Carhartt jacket. "What are you doing here?"

"Picking up my car."

"Now why would you want to do that?"

"So I can go back to Boston." First making a side trip, but he didn't share that information with Earl.

"Tomorrow is Christmas Eve," Earl said. "You got family in Boston?"

Flynn bit back his impatience at the change in subject. By now, he'd learned the only way to get a straight answer out of the auto mechanic was to take the Crazy Eights route. "All I have back there is an apartment and a doorman."

"A doorman?" Earl thought about that for a second. "Can't say I've ever heard of anyone having their doorman over for Christmas mornin'. He must be really good at opening your door."

Flynn sighed. This was going nowhere. "My car?"

"Oh, that. The part's on order."

"It hasn't arrived yet?"

"Oh, it arrived." Earl scratched under one earflap.

"And?"

"And I sent it back."

Flynn sighed again, this time longer and louder. "Why would you do that?"

"Because I'm getting old. Forgot my glasses on Tuesday."

Flynn resisted the urge to scream in frustration. "And what would that have to do with my car?"

"Made me order the wrong part. I got my two's all mixed up with my seven's. But don't you worry," Earl said, patting his breast pocket, "I brought my glasses today. So you'll be all set to leave by Friday at the latest."

"Can't you fix it now?"

"Nope. Gotta go work the tree lot at the Methodist church." Earl patted his hat down farther on the top of his head, then strode out of the shop, waving at Flynn to follow. "The ladies' bingo group is coming by at three to get their trees, and they're counting on my muscles to help them out. I can't be late."

Earl strode off, leaving Flynn stuck. He should have been mad. Should have pitched a fit, threatened to sue or have his car towed to another garage. He could have done any of the above.

But he didn't. For some reason, he wasn't as stressed about the missing part as he should have been. He chalked it up to still needing more information from Sam.

As his path carried him toward the bakery again, something pretty damned close to anticipation rose in his chest. If there was one thing Flynn needed from Santa this year, it was a renewed dose of his reporter's objectivity.

CHAPTER SEVEN

A PAY PHONE.

Who'd have thought those things still existed?

Flynn's hand rested on the receiver. Stumbling upon the phone on his way to the bakery had taken him by surprise. In his opposite hand, he jingled several coins, and debated. Finally, he picked up the phone, dropped in several quarters and began to dial. He made it through nine of the ten digits that would connect him to Liam's dorm room before he hung up.

It had to be this town that had him feeling so sentimental. Especially considering he was surrounded by so much Christmas spirit, it was like being in the company of a woman wearing too much perfume. Even the pay phone was wrapped in garland, a little red bow hanging from the handle. That must be what had him thinking of mending fences so broken down, it would take a fleet of cement trucks to build them up again.

Would Liam see him when he arrived in town this week? Assuming, that was, that his car ever got fixed. Or would Liam slam the door in his face? Maybe it was better not to know.

The change dropped to the bottom of the phone. Flynn dug it out of the slot and redeposited the coins, then added some more change to reach his editor at *Food Lovers* magazine.

But while he waited for the four dollars in quarters to connect him, he realized the money would have been better spent on a lifetime supply of candy canes. At least then he could have used them to sweeten Tony Reynolds up—

Because at this point he could use every tool in Santa's arsenal to assuage the inevitable storm that was about to come.

"Where the hell is that bakery piece?" Tony Reynolds barked into the phone. "We held the damned issue to get this piece in there because you promised to get it to me, remember? Or did you lose your brain back in June, too?"

Flynn winced. Even now, he couldn't tell Tony why he had walked out in the middle of the interview of the year, ticking off a celebrity chef. It was intended to be the cover story for the magazine, one they had advertised for the last three months, a coup that Tony had worked his butt off to finesse, promising the celebrity chef everything from a lifetime subscription to the magazine to a limo ride to the interview.

Flynn hadn't just dropped the ball at that interview—he'd hurled it through the window. He'd been working day and night to get back to the top ever since.

He hadn't expected to walk into that room, meet "Mondo," the chef to the stars, and see one of the first foster fathers he'd ever had. A man he and Liam had lived with for a total of six months before the man had decided the two boys were too much for the man and his wife, who were busy making a go of their restaurant, and he'd asked the department of children's services to find them another home.

The recognition had hit Flynn so hard, he'd never even made it into the room. Never said a word to the man. He'd made up some excuse to Tony about a bout of food poisoning, but the damage had been done. Mondo had stalked out of the building, furious about being stood up, and refused to reschedule.

Flynn had worked too damned hard building his reputation to let that one mistake ruin everything, which explained why he was the one out on assignment at Christmas while all the other writers were at home, toasting marshmallows or whatever people did with their families the day before Christmas Eve.

"I'll have the story," Flynn said. "You know I will."

"Yeah, I do. We're all allowed one mistake, huh?" Tony chuckled, calmer now that he'd blown off some steam. "You're the only guy who'll work on Christmas, too. Hell, you *never* take a day off. What is it, Flynn? You got some extra ambition gene the rest of us missed?"

"Maybe so." That drive to succeed had fueled him for so many years, had been a constantly burning fire, unquenchable by hundreds of cover stories, thousands of scoops. Then he'd faltered, and he'd been working himself to the bone to recover ever since. There'd be no messing up again. "I'll have the story, Tony," he repeated. "You can count on me."

"That's what makes you my personal Santa, Flynn." Tony laughed, then disconnected.

Flynn hung up the receiver. For a moment there, he'd let himself get sidetracked by Samantha Barnett. Hell, last night he'd even talked about *dating* her, got caught up in a whole champagne-and-lobster fantasy. No more.

He needed to eviscerate the emotion from this job. Get back to business. Then he could get out of this town, and get back to his priorities.

Sam hadn't spent this much time outside the bakery in…well, forever. She could thank Aunt

Ginny's matchmaking, though she didn't want to be matched with anyone at all, but she was grateful for the break from work. The minute Flynn MacGregor had entered Joyful Creations and said he needed to talk to her, Ginny had practically shoved Sam out the door and told the two of them to go ice skating.

"Do you know how to do this?" she asked Flynn.

He paused in lacing up the black skates. "Not really. Do you?"

"You can't grow up in rural Indiana without learning to ice skate. There's practically a pond in every backyard." She rose, balancing on her rented skates, then waited for Flynn to finish. Several dozen children and their parents were already skating on a small pond down the street from the park that was set up every winter as a makeshift rink.

He stood, teetering on the thin blades, reaching for the arms of the bench. "This isn't as easy as it looks."

She laughed. "Is anything ever as easy as it looks?"

"I suppose not." He rose again, then let go, taking his time until he was balanced. "Okay, I'm ready to go."

"If you've ever Rollerbladed before—" She cut off her words when she saw his dubious look. "Okay, so you're not the Rollerblading type."

"Limos, champagne and lobster, remember?"

Oh, yeah. She remembered. Very well. In fact, she hadn't been thinking of much but that since their date—no, it hadn't been a date, had it?—last night.

They made their way through the compacted snow on the bank and down to the ice. Sam stepped onto the rink first, then put out her hand. Flynn hesitated for a second, then took her hand and joined her, with a lot of wobbling. Even through two pairs of gloves—his and hers—a surge of electricity ran up Sam's arm when Flynn touched her. This was *so* not in the plan for the day.

"Okay, so where do we start?" he asked. "Hopefully, it's not a position that lands me on my butt."

She laughed. "I can't promise that."

"Then I can't promise to be nice in my article."

She couldn't tell if he was joking or not. She hoped he was. But just in case, she held on to him, even as part of her told her to let go, because every touch awakened a stirring of feelings she hadn't expected. "First, pretend you're on a scooter. Take a step, glide, take a step, glide. Put your arms in front of you to balance."

He let go of her and did as she said, while Sam skated backward, a few feet before him. He wobbled back and forth, scowling at first, frustrated with the whole process. "I give up."

She laughed. "So soon?"

He swayed like a palm tree in a hurricane. "You said you wouldn't let me—"

She caught him just before he fell, the two of them colliding together in that close—very, very close—position of the dancing he had mentioned last night. Hyperawareness pulsed through her, and she tried to pull back, but Flynn's balance still depended on her, and she found her body fitting into the crook of his, as naturally as a missing puzzle piece.

"Fall," he finished, his voice low and husky.

"I didn't," she answered, nearly in a whisper.

He bent down to look at her, his mouth inches from hers, and Sam held her breath, desire coursing through her, the heat overriding the cold air. "Thank you."

"You're…you're welcome."

A crowd of teenagers whipped past them, laughing and chattering, their loud voices jerking Sam back to reality. She inserted some distance between them, locking her arms to keep herself from closing that space again.

"Let's try this again," Flynn said. He started moving forward, one scoot at a time, while Sam slid backward, her gaze first on their feet, and the milky white surface holding them up, then, as Flynn began to master the movement, she allowed her gaze to travel up, connecting with him.

He was intoxicating. Tempting. Her skate skipped across a dent in the ice, and she tripped. Flynn's grip tightened on hers. "Careful," he said.

"I'm trying," Sam said. Trying her best.

"Do you do this often?"

They swished around the rink, going in a wide circle, circumventing the other skaters with an easy shift of hips. "Not often enough. I love to skate. Love the outdoors."

"You? An outdoorsy girl?"

She laughed. "I didn't say I was Outdoorsy Girl, but I do like to do things outside. Garden, skate, swim."

"Swim?" Heat rose in his gaze, the kind that told her he was picturing her in a swimsuit, imagining her body in the water. Another wave of desire coursed through Sam.

"You must have gone swimming a lot, growing up near an ocean."

A shadow dropped over his face. "I used to. But then I…moved."

"Oh." Flynn didn't seem to want to continue that line of questions, so Sam moved on. "What made you get into writing about restaurants?" She grinned. "Do you just like food?"

"I do," he acknowledged. Flynn began to glide forward, his steps becoming a little surer, even as his conversation stayed at a near standstill. "As to the restaurant business, I have some personal acquaintance with it."

Something cold and distant had entered Flynn's gaze, like a wall sliding between them. Not that he'd ever been that open to begin with, but Sam had begun to feel like they were sort of making headway, and now—

He had gone back to being as impersonal as that first day. Was it because the issue wasn't with her…

But with him?

"What happened in your life?" she asked, emotionally and physically invading his space by sliding her body a little closer, not letting him back down this time, or back away. She sensed a chink in his armor, a slight open window, something that told her there was more to Flynn MacGregor than a man who didn't want to sing "Jingle Bells."

"Nothing."

"I don't believe you. And I don't believe all that hooey about seeing one too many restaurateurs give up their lives to their restaurants. This all seems so personal to you, Flynn. Why?"

Sam was sure, given the choice, he would have moved away, but he was stuck on the ice, stuck holding on to her. He paused a long time, so long she wasn't sure he was going to answer. "I know someone who chose their business over their family."

"Over…you?"

Flynn swung his body to the side, breaking eye contact. He had clear natural athletic ability, which had allowed him to pick up the ice skating quickly, and he let go of one of her hands. "I'm not in Riverbend to talk about me."

"Does every second of our time together have to be about the article?"

"No." But he didn't elaborate. Another group of teenagers whooshed past them, their raucous noise a stark contrast to the tight tension between Flynn and Sam.

She sighed. He was as closemouthed as a snapping turtle. Why? Perhaps she had treaded too close to very personal waters. Could she really blame him for pushing her off? If he had started asking about her grandmother, she would have likely done the same. "I guess it's not too fun to be on the other end of the interview, huh?"

A slight grin quirked up one side of his mouth. "It's not a position I like being in, no."

"Join the club. I know it's good for business and all, but…" She toed at the ice, stopping one skate so that she swung around to skate beside him instead of in front of him, figuring then he'd let go of her hand, but he didn't. "But it's uncomfortable all the same."

"Why?"

"I'm afraid I'll say something I'll regret. And you—" She cut the words off.

"And I'll what?"

Sam cursed the slip of tongue. Now she had to answer. "You'll write one of those tabloid type stories."

"The ones the magazine, and I, am known for."

She watched the ice pass beneath her, solid and hard, cold. "Yes."

"You don't trust me?"

She glanced at him. "Should I?"

The same group of teenagers hurried past them, one brushing past Flynn, causing him to wobble. "Let's take a break for a little while."

"Sure." They made their way off the ice and over to the park bench where they had stored their shoes. The bench sat beneath two trees, long bared by winter's cold. Before them, the skaters continued in repeating circles.

As soon as they sat down on the small bench, the tiny seat making for tight quarters, the tension between them ratcheted up another couple of notches. Sam wished for someone else to come along and defuse the situation. For the teens to rush by, for Aunt Ginny to pop out of the woods, for Earl to amble by, heck, anyone.

"Listen, ah, I didn't mean to pry," she said, diverting back to the earlier topic. It would be best not to make an enemy of this man. "Your personal life is your own."

"And I didn't mean to bite your head off. I'm just not used to women who take such an interest in me personally."

"I'm not, I mean…" She felt her face heat again. Damn. Why did he have to look at her so directly, with those blue X-ray eyes? "What are they interested in?"

"Let me put it this way. They're not looking for deep, meaningful relationships when they date me."

"And neither are you?"

He chuckled. "No. That's not me, at all."

"Oh." Disappointment settled in her stomach. She couldn't have said why. For one, he was here as a reporter, not as a potential boyfriend. For another, Flynn MacGregor was leaving town in a day, maybe two, and he wasn't the kind who believed in permanence, settling down.

Besides, when did she have time to do either? She couldn't have a relationship, even if she wanted to. Guilt pricked at her conscience, for even thinking she could. She had priorities. Priorities that did not include a man.

Yet, he was tempting, very much so, especially when he was this close. She could see why women would be attracted to him. He had a curious mix of mystery and charm, of aloofness, yet a hint of vulnerability, as if there was something there, something wounded, that he was trying to cover.

"I'm just not the settling down kind," Flynn said. "And most of the women I date understand that." He draped one arm over the back of the bench, then leaned a little closer to Sam. "But I bet you aren't like that at all, are you? The kind that would understand a guy like me."

"We may be more alike than you think," she said quietly.

"You think so?"

She could only nod in response. The noise of the skaters on the pond seemed to disappear, the world becoming just the two of them.

"Maybe you're right." His voice was deep, the timbre seeming to reach crevices in Sam's heart that hadn't been touched in a long time. And all he'd said was three words.

Geez. She really needed to get out more.

Flynn closed the gap between them. For the first time, Sam noticed how the light blue of his dress shirt seemed to make the blue of his eyes richer, deeper. Her pulse began to race, thudding through her veins. "There's only one way to find out."

Sam swallowed hard, her heart beating so loud, she was sure Flynn could hear the pounding. "Find out what?"

"If you would be interested in me."

He caught a tendril of her hair between his gloved fingers, letting it slip through the leather. "We've been dancing around the subject all week."

"Have we?" she asked, the slight catch of laughter in her voice, a clear giveaway of her nerves. "Or is this…"

"What?" he prompted.

"Nothing," she said, not wanting to voice her greatest fear, not wanting to break the sweet, yet dangerous tension.

The silence between them stretched one second. Two. Three. Heat filled the few inches separating them, building like a fever. Sam gazed up at Flynn, her breath caught somewhere in her throat, as if her lungs had forgotten their job. He released her hair, then pulled off his glove and cupped her jaw, using the same hand that had slid down her zipper. A hundred times over the last couple of days she had stolen glimpses of his hands, fascinated by the definition of his fingers, the implied power in his grip, and now, now, he was touching her, just as she'd pictured, and she leaned into the touch, into his thumb tracing along her bottom lip, the desire building and building.

Flynn leaned forward. Slow. Tentative. Taking his time. Because he was unsure? Waiting for her response? His gaze never left hers. Then his fingers slipped down to her neck, dancing along the sensitive skin of her throat—

And he kissed her.

CHAPTER EIGHT

FLYNN HADN'T INTENDED to kiss Samantha Barnett—he could honestly say in all the years he had covered the restaurant business that he had never kissed anyone that he had interviewed. But something had come over him, and the temptation to taste those lips—to see if his theory about neither of them being interested in the other would hold up—had overwhelmed him.

He knew it wasn't her grandmother's cookies; he hadn't even eaten any of those. And either way, truth be told, he'd wanted to kiss Sam pretty much from minute one. Okay, maybe minute two. And now that he finally had—

The experience had lived up to his every expectation. And then some. Kissing Samantha Barnett was like coming home, only Flynn had never really experienced a home, just dreamed of one. She was soft, and welcoming, warm and giving, and yet, she inspired a passion in him, a craving, for more.

But that would be unwise. He was a bulldog, the one who got the article at all costs, not the puppy cowed by a sweet treat.

So Flynn pulled back. "That, ah, won't be part of the article."

"Good." Sam let out a little laugh. "I definitely don't need Bakery Owner Kisses Reporter in Exchange for Good PR as part of the headline." She traced a line along the edge of the painted green bench. "Then what was that? Research?"

He chuckled. When was the last time he'd laughed, really laughed? Hell, if he couldn't remember, then it had definitely been too long. Sam was intoxicating, in more ways than one, and that was dangerous ground to tread. "No, not part of the research. Though, if there is a line of work that lets me kiss you as part of my job—"

"Sorry, no. I'm not part of anyone's resume."

"Pity. And here I was all ready to fill out a job application, too."

What was he saying? He needed to grab hold of his objectivity, and not let go.

A smile slid across her lips, and something that approached joy ballooned in Flynn's chest. The feeling was foreign, new. "You're turning into a joke a minute, Flynn MacGregor. Before you know it, you'll be appearing on a late night comedy special."

"Oh, yeah, that's me. Flynn the comic." He

chuckled. Again. Twice in the space of one minute. That had to be an all-time personal record.

He watched her join him in laughter, and the temptation to kiss her again rose inside him, fast and furious. Flynn jerked his attention away and began to unlace his skates. "I should probably get back to work."

"All work and no play?"

He looked up at her. "I could say the same for you."

"Oh, I play. Sometimes."

"When?" He moved closer to her, ignoring the warning bells in his head reminding him he should be working, not flirting. "Is there a non-business side to Samantha Barnett?"

It was a pure research question. The kind he could use to delve deeper, expose a vulnerable vein. He'd done it a hundred times—

Except this time he found his attention not on how he would write up her answer, or what his next question would be, but on whether her answer would be something that would interest him, too. Something they could do together.

She brushed her bangs out of her face, revealing more of her heart-shaped countenance. "Well, Christmas, for sure. I love this time of year."

"I think it's a prerequisite for living in this town."

"You might learn to love the holiday, too," she said. "In fact, if you're looking for something to cultivate your feelings for Christmas, you could go to the Riverbend Winterfest."

"Winterfest?"

Sam nodded, her eyes shining with excitement, a fever Flynn could almost imagine catching. "The town recently started holding this really big Christmas celebration. C. J. Hamilton does it up big, bringing in all kinds of decorations and moving props. He dresses up as Santa, and his wife is Mrs. Claus. Even Earl gets into the spirit. This year, I hear he's dressing up as an elf and handing out candy canes to all the kids who come to Santa's workshop. That alone should be worth the price of admission, which is free anyway. It's a really fun time."

What it sounded like was another date. Another temptation. Another opportunity to be alone with Samantha Barnett.

And a bad idea.

"It's, ah, not really my cup of tea. Besides, I should probably be working on my article." He slipped off his skates and put his shoes back on, as a visual and physical reminder of getting out of here.

"The Winterfest starts at night. You have plenty of time to do your article and anything else you might want to accomplish today." She took off her own skates, then met his gaze. He found himself watching her mouth move, fantasizing about kissing her again. And again. "You should reconsider. You'll be missing something really cool. Trust me, Winterfest is fun for more than just kids. I love going."

"I'm not much of a Christmas person."

"Oh. Well, it was just an idea."

"I didn't mean to offend you."

"You didn't." She tied her skates together, then slid her feet into her boots.

"It's just..." He paused. "Where I grew up, Christmas wasn't a big deal."

Sam smiled. "When I was a kid, Christmas was the biggest day of the year. My family was total Christmas-holics, and after my parents died, my grandmother did Christmas up even bigger, as if to make up for losing my mother and father." Her smile died on her lips, and her gaze drifted to the skaters rounding the rink. "I miss those days."

"What happened?"

"My grandmother isn't there like she used to be."

Flynn opened his mouth, as if he intended to ask her what she meant by that, then closed it again. Sam regretted saying anything at all. She had done her best to keep her grandmother's condition private, from everyone in town. Not just to protect Grandma Joy, but to prevent the in-evitable questions. The visitors who would stop by to see Joy, and be hurt that she didn't know them. The pity parties, the people who wanted to help lift the burden from Sam's shoulders.

No one understood this burden couldn't be lifted. Her grandmother didn't remember her. Didn't know her. No amount of sympathy would ever change that.

So Sam kept the details to herself, told people Joy was happily living a life at a retirement home, and buried herself in her work. Carrying on her family's legacy, living up to generations of expectations—not from her grandmother, but from this town. There'd been a Barnett behind the stove at Joyful Creations since it had opened, and that's what customers expected when they walked in the door.

Even if a part of Sam wanted to walk out that door one day and keep on walking. To pretend that she didn't have those responsibilities waiting for her every morning. To imagine a different life, one that was more—

Complete.

"This Winterfest thing is probably the social event of the year, huh?" Flynn said, drawing Sam out of her thoughts.

"It is. People look forward to it. Myself included." She laughed. "I spend days baking like crazy before it, to supply the festival's stand, while a few people work the downtown shop. We get a lot of out-of-towners for Winterfest, so it's a busy day for all the stores around here." Sam rose and put a fist on her hip. "It's a big deal, for those who dare to go. So, do you?"

One corner of Flynn's mouth curved up. "Are you challenging me?" He took a few steps closer, the distance between them shrinking from feet to inches in an instant. He flipped at the laces on her skates, dangling from her fingers, hanging near her hips. Sam inhaled and her breath caught in her throat, held, waiting, for—

What? For Flynn to make a move? For him to kiss her again?

Oh, how she wished he would, even as another part of her wished he wouldn't.

He distracted her, awakened her to the possibilities she had laid aside for so long. He had this way of forcing her to open her eyes, to confront issues she'd much rather leave at the door.

"I am," she said, the two words nearly a breath.

"I should…" Flynn began, his body so close she could feel the heat emanating from his skin, and the answering heat rising inside her. Then the grin widened, and before Sam could second-guess her challenge, it was too late. "Suddenly I can't think of anything else I should do, but go with you."

CHAPTER NINE

FLYNN SHOULD HAVE put the pieces together sooner. He used to be really good at that. Figuring out what parts of the story people held back. And why.

But this time, his objectivity had been compromised. By his attraction to Sam? By the town? By that one assignment going so horribly awry? Whatever it was, Flynn had lost his tight hold on his life, and that had caused him to stop paying attention to the details.

Until now.

Until he'd returned to the bed and breakfast after ice skating, and Betsy Williams had started chatting up a storm, first pointing out a photo on the wall of Sam and her grandmother, then telling tales about the two of them working together, then finally segueing into rumors about the cookies.

"You wouldn't believe how fast people are

eating those cookies up," Betsy was saying as Flynn helped her carry the dishes out to the dining room table and set up for dinner.

Betsy had pronounced Flynn a "sweet boy" for volunteering, having no idea of his ulterior motive. How many times had he employed a similar tactic? Using a nice gesture as a way to get more information out of someone? Never before had it bothered him. He was doing his job, just as he should. But today, every dish he carried, every fork he laid on the table, while Betsy chattered on, seemed to nag at him, like stones on his back.

"I feel like I'm running *The Dating Game* right in my little B and B," Betsy went on. "Maybe I should open a wedding chapel next door." She laughed. "Oh, wouldn't Sam's grandmother get such a kick out of this, if she could see what was happening with that bakery."

"Where is Sam's grandmother, by the way?"

Betsy shut the door of the dining room hutch and turned back to Flynn, a silver bread platter in her hands. "She didn't tell you?"

Flynn shrugged, feigning nonchalance. "We didn't talk much about her."

"Oh, well, that's because Sam hardly ever talks about Joy. No one in this town does, either, though they like to speculate, being a small town and all."

"Why?"

"Well…" Betsy looked around, as if she expected Sam to appear in the dining room at any second. "I don't know the whole story, but I heard from Estelle, who heard from Carolyn, who heard from Louise, that Joy isn't really living at a retirement home and playing golf every day."

A tide rose in Flynn's chest. This was the missing piece, the nugget he searched for in every story, the one that made headlines, the one that earned his reputation on every article. He could feel it, with an instinct bred from years on the job. "Really? Where is she?"

"No one's really sure because we never see Joy anymore, and if you ask Sam or Ginny, they just put on a brave face and keep on sticking to that retirement home story. But you know…" Again, Betsy looked around, then returned her attention to Flynn. "Before she 'retired,' Joy was getting real forgetful. Doing things like wandering around town in her nightgown, showing up to work at the bakery in the middle of the night, telling Earl, a man she's known all her life, that she didn't know him. We just thought she was overworked, you know? That bakery, it's a handful, I'm sure. I know, because I have this bed and breakfast. It's a lot for one woman."

The pieces of the story assembled in Flynn's head, and he could nearly write the article already, see the bold letters of the headline leaping from the pages. His editor would be crowing with joy when this came across the transom. "You think Joy went to a home for people with Alzheimer's?"

"Maybe. I mean, where else could she be? And that leaves poor Sam with hardly no family, except for her Aunt Ginny." Betsy pressed a hand to her heart. She sighed, then looked back at the photo on the wall, taken outside of Joyful Creations. "Well, she does have that shop. That place has been her real family, for a long time. And you know, I think that's the saddest part of all."

A couple burst through the bed and breakfast's doors just then, giggling and feeding each other bites of the special cherry chocolate chunk cookies. The reporter in Flynn knew his job was to pursue that couple—they personified the kind of happily-ever-after that would be perfect for his article—but another part of him was still tuned to Betsy's words, even as she said something about getting pies in the oven and hurried off to the kitchen.

Flynn pulled his notepad out of his back pocket, and took two steps toward the couple. Then he paused, stopping by the black-and-white photograph of Sam and her grandmother, one photo among the several dozen crowding Betsy's wall. Even back then, Sam was smiling, beaming, really, with pride, standing beneath the curved banner of the store's name. And the woman beside her, an older version of Sam, reflected the same joy and pride.

Flynn's notepad weighed heavy in his palm. He knew where the rest of his story lay. The problem?

Deciding whether it would be worth the price he'd pay to go after it.

"We fell in love, just like that." The couple beamed and leaned into each other, looking so happy, they could have been an ad for a jewelry store.

Flynn had spent his afternoon tracking down couples who attributed their romances to the legendary cherry chocolate chunk cookies from Joyful Creations. The process had been easy. After talking to the duo at the bed and breakfast, he'd simply asked Betsy for recommendations. One chat led to another and to another. In a small town, just about everyone had a neighbor, a sister, a friend who believed the treats were the reason for their marital bliss.

Every single one of them thanked the legendary Joy Barnett for their bliss. They extolled the virtues of Sam, for carrying on Joy's legacy, during Joy's retirement.

Retirement.

There was no retirement, of that Flynn was sure. Every reporter's instinct he had told him so. Sam was trying to keep the truth the secret.

The question was why.

Finding that out would make for an interesting story. A very interesting story, indeed.

"Did you know the cookies were supposed to make people fall in love?" he asked.

"Well, it wasn't a *known* fact," the woman said, "not until the magazine story came out. But now everyone in Riverbend knows. And, all over the country, too."

"So this was just kind of a coincidence?"

"Not at all. We went out on a date, we had cookies and we fell in love."

Flynn kept himself from saying anything about the possibility that a sugar high might have led to a hasty infatuation. He just jotted down the quote, thanked the couple for their time and left their small Cape house. The snow had frozen enough to keep from soaking his pants and shoes as he walked through the streets of Riverbend and back to the bakery to meet Sam. He had everything he needed for his article—

Except the story of Sam's grandmother.

He could, of course, write the article without it. Just turn around, go back to the bed and breakfast, plug in what he had and leave it at that. But it wouldn't be the article his editor was expecting, nor would it be the kind of article he was known for.

Flynn MacGregor didn't quit until he got to the real story. He made a lot of enemies that way, but he also made a lot of reader fans, and a hell of a lot of money.

The magazine was called *Food Lovers* because its readers loved to know the real story behind the food. They didn't just want recipes and tips on choosing a knife; they wanted to know what kind of childhood their favorite chef had, or whether that restaurant failed because the hostess divorced the owner.

And that meant Flynn would find out what happened to Sam's grandmother. He'd want to know—because his readers would eat it up. Pun intended.

Since Sam had agreed to meet Flynn downtown, he stopped by the pay phone again. His cell still wasn't having any luck finding a signal, and calling from Betsy's meant using the public phone in the front parlor—with the carolers hanging on his every word.

So he deposited his change into the public phone, and dialed Mimi's number. On the other end, three rings, then a distracted, "Hello?"

"Mimi? It's Flynn."

The sounds of music, laughing and bubbly

conversation carried over the line, nearly drowning out Mimi's response. "Flynn MacGregor, I can't believe you didn't show up at my Christmas party. Didn't even RSVP. That's so totally rude."

"I told you, I had to go out of town on assignment."

Mimi let out a gust. "Again? You know I can never keep track of your schedule."

"I don't expect you to." But a part of him was disappointed that once again, Mimi hadn't paid attention. Hadn't even cared.

Sam wouldn't do that to someone. Sam would have noticed. Sam would have baked him a box of cookies to take along for the ride, for Pete's sake.

Where did that come from? He didn't need a woman like Sam. He liked his life unencumbered. He could come and go as he pleased. No one waiting for him, no one expecting him to make a home, settle down.

"Listen, Flynn, I can't talk right now. I have, like, fifty people here." Then Mimi was gone, the congestion of people silenced with a click.

"Everything okay back in Boston?"

Flynn turned. Sam stood behind him, bundled as always in her thick, marshmallowlike jacket. Mimi, who followed every fashion tip espoused by the editors of *Vogue*, would never have worn anything even close. She preferred sleek, impractical coats in a rainbow of colors that accented her attire like diamonds on a necklace. "It's the same as always," he said.

"Ready to go to the Winterfest?"

Flynn would have rather taken a dip in Boston Harbor than spend his evening at the town's homage to all things Christmas. But what else did he have to do? Spending a little more time with Samantha Barnett could only help him fill in those few more details he wanted. Maybe get her to open up, tell him about her grandmother without him having to probe.

Hell, who was he kidding?

The details Flynn was interested in had less to do with his article and more to do with the way she filled out her sweater, the way her smile curved across her face, and the way her laughter seemed to draw him in and make him wonder if maybe he'd been missing out on something for the last thirty years of his life.

Even as he told himself not to get emotionally involved, to hold himself back.

Not to make the same mistake twice.

They headed down the sidewalk, past several shops that were so decorated for Christmas, they could have been advertisements for the holiday. A toy store, a deli, a church. On every light pole hung a red banner advertising the Riverbend

Winterfest, while white lights sparkled in the branches of tiny saplings that lined the street. People hurried by them, chattering about Christmas, while children stopped to peer into the windows of the shops, their hands cupped over their eyes to see deeper inside.

Flynn took Sam's hand. It seemed a natural thing to do, something dozens of other couples were doing. She glanced over at him, a slight look of surprise on her face, but didn't pull away. His larger palm engulfed hers, yet a tingle of warm electricity sizzled up his arm at her touch.

"This way." She tugged him down a side street. When he turned, he saw the park where he'd seen the live reindeer earlier. Only now it had been transformed into a mega-winter wonderland with the atmosphere of a carnival, taken to the nth degree. The grassy area was filled with people, and looked like something straight out of a movie. Hundreds of lighted Christmas displays, featuring every image associated with the holiday that a human being could imagine and hook up to ten gazillion watts, ringed the central gazebo, while little stands from local vendors sold everything from Riverbend T-shirts to hot pretzels.

Sam stopped walking and let out a sigh. "Isn't it perfect? It's like every child's dream of the perfect Christmas day."

And it was. At one end, by a small shed, Santa

Claus held court, with Mrs. Claus by his side. To the right, the live reindeer was in his pen, chomping a carrot. On the roof of the shed, someone had installed a lighted sleigh and eight painted fake reindeer. He bit back a laugh. "You weren't lying, were you?"

"I told you he was dressing up as an elf."

Earl Klein, in an oversized elf costume, looking more like the Jolly Green Giant than one of Santa's helpers, stood to the front of the small shed, handing out candy canes and greeting all the children. Throughout the park, a sound system played a jaunty, tinny selection of Christmas carols, carrying through the air with the scent of hot chocolate and peppermint. Hundreds of people milled around the Winterfest, chatting happily, visiting the petting zoo, greeting old friends, hugging family members.

"People really get into this thing, don't they?"

"I told you, it's a big deal."

"It's…unbelievable."

Sam laughed. "No, it's fun, that's what it is."

Everything Sam had promised him was here. The Riverbend Winterfest was, indeed, the perfect Christmas celebration, all in one place.

"Let's hit the games first. There's a prize every time." Sam pointed toward a set of dart games, with stuffed animal prizes dangling from the roof. "How's your aim?"

He chuckled. "Terrible."

"Good thing there's a prize every time then."

Before he could protest, or think twice, Flynn found himself plunking down a couple bucks to throw a trio of darts at some small balloons. A few minutes later, he was rewarded with a tiny stuffed Santa, which he handed to Sam. "Your prize, m'lady."

"Oh, it's all yours. A souvenir from your time in Riverbend."

He ticktocked the miniature jolly guy back and forth. "He'd be my one and only Christmas decoration."

Sam closed her hand over his, and over the toy. "Well, you gotta start somewhere, don't you?"

Did he? Flynn stuffed the toy in his pocket, more disconcerted than he could remember being before. And all over a Santa no bigger than the palm of his hand. This was crazy.

He walked through the displays, tasting the pretzels, riding on a few of the rides, with Sam by his side, telling himself he should be asking her questions, probing deeper for his article, but he kept getting distracted…by the one thing he'd never thought he'd find in this town.

A good time.

They paused by the Joyful Creations booth, manned by Sam's Aunt Ginny. "Well, hello there. Are you two having a good time?"

"We are," Sam answered, sparing Flynn.

"Would you like to try some cookies?" her aunt asked, holding up a platter. "The shop's specialty, perhaps?"

Sam shot her a glare.

"No, I'm good. Thank you." After interviewing that couple earlier, Flynn wasn't taking any chances on having those cherry chocolate chunk cookies. Not that he believed the rumors, but—

Just in case.

Turning his life upside down by falling in love would be completely insane. So he'd stick to the story, and avoid the desserts. Yep. That was the plan. Except…

He wasn't doing so well in that department thus far. He couldn't help but admire Sam's curves, the way her hair danced around her shoulders as he followed her away from the booth and over to the carousel, where they stood and watched some children ride wooden ponies in a circle.

"There's something I've been meaning to ask you," Sam said.

"Shoot."

"Boston's really far from Indiana. Did you really drive all the way out here, just to interview me?"

"Well…not exactly."

"What do you mean?" They started walking

again, weaving in and out among the crowds, the scents of hot chocolate, peppermint and popcorn wrapping around them like a blanket.

"I drove so I had the freedom to make another stop." Assuming, that was, that he was welcome.

"To visit family?"

Flynn shrugged. "Something like that."

"Do you have much family back home in Boston?"

The fun moments they'd been having dissolved as quickly as snow under direct sunlight. "No." He paused. "Yes."

Why hadn't he stopped at no? Where had that compulsion to qualify his answer come from? Now he was opening a door he had kept shut for years. A door he had never opened to anyone else.

"Yes and no?" She smiled. "Now, that's an interesting family."

"My brother used to live there…but we don't talk." That was an understatement and a half. Flynn could have said more, but he didn't. Why and how he and Liam had drifted apart required starting at the beginning, and Flynn refused to go back there. For anyone.

"Oh. I'm sorry."

"Yeah."

Whoa, there was an answer, Flynn. He could see the question marks in Sam's eyes, the inevitable "why" lingering in her gaze, but she didn't voice the question, and he didn't volunteer the answer.

He paused beside a hayride station, watching the children in line, thinking Sam would let the conversation go. Hoping she would. But when he racked his brain for another topic, he came up with…nothing.

"Older or younger?" she asked.

"What do you mean?"

"Is your brother older or younger? I'm an only child, so I've never had a sibling." She sighed. "I always wondered what it would be like, though I had cousins around a lot when I was a kid. They were sort of like brothers and sisters."

"He's younger. In his last year of college."

"Wow. A lot younger, huh?"

"Just four years. He got a late start on going to Purdue." What was this, show-and-tell? He'd never told anyone this much about Liam—ever. Yet, Sam's openness, her friendly, easy questions, made talking about his brother seem like the most natural thing in the world. Like he had a normal background. A normal family. A normal personal story to tell. Like so many of the ones surrounding them.

When the truth was completely the opposite.

"He's at Purdue? But, that's not far from here."

"I know."

"You could stop and see him for the holidays. The drive isn't too bad, maybe an hour and a half…" Her voice trailed off as she read his face, which must have said he wasn't going to go down that conversational road, because he'd already visited it and turned around. "You probably know that, too."

"I do."

Let the topic drop, he thought. Don't press it. He didn't want to talk about Liam, because doing that would lead to a conversation about his past. And that wasn't a door he wanted to open.

But Sam apparently didn't possess mind-reading skills.

"If your brother is still in school, then he's probably not married, is he?" Then she paused, and a blush filled her face. "I never thought to ask if you were. I just assumed, because you kissed me…"

"I'm not married." They stopped at a snack stand and ordered two coffees to go. "Not now. Not then, and not ever. I'm not a marrying kind of guy."

She cocked an elbow on the counter and tossed him a grin. "What's the matter? Are you scared of the big, bad altar?"

"No. It's just…" This time, he did have the sense to cut himself off before he started opening any more painful doors. He handed her a foam cup, then took his and started walking again.

"Just what?"

He took a long gulp of the coffee. The hot caffeine nearly seared his throat. "Some of us are meant for settling down, and some aren't."

"The nomadic freelancer?"

"Something like that."

Sam tipped her head and studied him, apparently not put off by his short answers. "Funny, it's hard to see you as a nomad."

He snorted. "You think I'm some two-point-five kids, German-shepherd-in-the-suburbs guy?"

"I think…you'd fit into a town like this better than you think." Her green eyes pierced through the shell that Flynn thought had been like steel-plated armor, but apparently, around her, had a few unprotected areas. "And that you're secretly more of a golden retriever guy."

"You have the golden retriever part right." He got to his feet. "But I'd never fit into a place like this. And I know that from personal experience."

He knew the truth. And knew he couldn't keep on walking around this Winterfest and pretend he was part of that world. That he could be some normal family guy, like all the others he saw. Sipping cocoa, laughing, singing. Acting like this was just another merry Christmas, one more out of dozens.

Whereas Flynn had never learned to have one

in the first place. He tossed his half-full coffee into a nearby trash can.

"I have to go. I have work to do," Flynn said. "Sorry."

She pivoted toward him. The tease was still in her eyes, because she didn't understand, didn't see what this would cost him. How he couldn't experience this, and then walk away from it at the end.

It would have been better not to go at all.

"Not so fast, mister," she said. "There's more to this than just you not wanting to play pin-the-nose-on-Rudolph, isn't there?"

Flynn glanced over his shoulder at the Christmas paradise. The music and the scents streamed outward, calling to him like a siren. "I'm just not in the mood for holly jolly right now. I have work to do."

Then he left, before he could be tempted into something he knew he'd regret, by a woman who was surrounded by a cloud of cinnamon and vanilla. A woman who made all of that seem so possible—when Flynn knew the truth.

CHAPTER TEN

SAM HAD TO BE CRAZY.

Here she was, walking the streets of Riverbend long after the Winterfest had ended. Her breath escaped her in bursts of white clouds, and though she had her hood up and her coat zipped all the way to the neck, the cold still managed to seep through the thick fabric. If she was smart, she'd go home and go to sleep. After all, she had to be up bright and early tomorrow morning to start baking, and begin the whole vicious work cycle all over again.

Just as she had every day of her life for the past umpteen years.

But after leaving the Winterfest, still confused about Flynn's early exit, she'd headed back to the house where she'd grown up. Once there, a restlessness had invaded her, and she'd been unable to sleep. She'd paced for half an hour, then finally given up, slipped back into her coat and boots and headed out into the cold.

The bracing winter air stung her cheeks like icy mosquitoes, while the dryness sucked the moisture from her lips, but she kept walking, increasing her stride. Silence blanketed Riverbend, with all the residents snug in their proverbial beds. Sam loved this time of day, when she could be alone, with her thoughts, her town, herself. Her steps faltered when she noticed a familiar figure outlined under the warm glow of a porch light.

Flynn.

Apparently she wasn't the only one who couldn't sleep.

Sam hesitated, then strode up the walkway of Betsy's Bed and Breakfast. "I thought a good night's sleep was guaranteed."

He scoffed. "Guess I better ask Betsy for a refund."

"Well," Sam began, suddenly uncomfortable under his piercing blue gaze, "I suppose I should get back to my walk."

"At this hour? Isn't that a little dangerous?"

She laughed. "In Riverbend? Our crime rate is so low, it's not even a number."

He shook his head. "I didn't think places like that existed."

"Walk with me, and you can see for yourself."

What had made her offer that? She'd gone out with the express intention of being alone. And here she'd gone and invited Flynn MacGregor along. The more time she spent with this man, the more she revealed about herself. Too much time, and she'd be exposing secrets she didn't want in print.

He was in town for one reason—for a story, and nothing more. Tonight, after she'd gone home, she'd unearthed some back issues of *Food Lovers* that had sat in her den, unread for months and months. Sam had skimmed them and found exactly what Aunt Ginny had said— most of the articles were more focused on the personal lives of their subjects than their products or business.

Sam's heart had sunk. Even as she knew better, she'd hoped for something different. Many of the articles had had Flynn MacGregor's byline. The worst ones, in fact. The ones that were the harshest, the ones that had the most blaring head-lines about businesses rocked by divorces, by deaths of a partner or a hidden bankruptcy.

And now, she knew, she'd end up the same way.

He wasn't really interested in her. How could she think anything different? He was using the kisses, using his charm, for one reason only.

To get the story.

He was a reporter.

Not a friend.

Just because he'd kissed her, and she'd kissed him back, didn't change anything.

Except…it did. She found herself liking him, even despite knowing all this. She sensed something about him, a vulnerability. It pulled at Sam, and told her there was a story beneath him, too. The problem was whether she was willing to take the risk of getting close to him to find out what that story was.

"A walk sounds good," Flynn said, ending Sam's internal debate. "It'll let me see the town with new eyes."

Maybe this wouldn't be such a bad idea after all. Perhaps if she showed him a softer, quieter side of town, he'd feature Riverbend in his article—and not her.

Uh-huh. And maybe she was just some naive country bumpkin, after all.

Flynn rose, buttoned his coat tighter against the cold, then hurried down the stairs. "Promise not to drag me to any hometown festivals? Or force me to ooh and ahh over the decorations?"

Sam crossed her heart. "Scout's honor."

A slight smile played on his lips. "Were you ever a Girl Scout?"

"Four years. I had to drop out because I needed to help in the bakery after school." They began to walk, falling into stride together. The town was silent, save for the occasional car or barking dog. Beneath their feet, snow crunched like corn-flakes in a cereal bowl. "How about you? Were you ever in Boy Scouts?"

"No. I never…had time."

The pause in the middle of the sentence made her wonder. What was he leaving out? But he didn't seem inclined to share, and she couldn't badger him when she didn't want him to do the same to her, so she let it go.

Just as he had at the Winterfest, Flynn's hand dropped down and sought hers again, and he held onto her as they walked. It seemed so normal, so wonderful, and yet, she tried not to enjoy the feeling, tried to remind herself that he wasn't staying and she didn't have time for a relationship.

And most of all, that Flynn had ulterior motives for getting close to her.

Above them, heavy snow creaked in the branches of the trees, threatening to break under the extra weight. An SUV passed them, its tires crunching on the icy roads, red lights winking when the car turned right.

"I love the houses when they're decorated for the holidays." Sam sighed. "It looks so… magical."

Flynn glanced up at the cascade of lights around them. Had he ever taken the time to notice Christmas lights before? The way they twinkled in the ebony darkness? The play of white and red against shrubs and siding, the dancing rainbow of bulbs running along gutters, edging the houses with an almost mystical brilliance? "They're… nice. I guess."

Okay, they were *very* nice, but he kept that to himself. He refused to fall in love with this town, because places like this—seasons like this— didn't last.

"When I was little, my father hated hanging the lights, or at least that's what he always said. I think it's because he took them down so fast at the end of the year, they were a jumbled mess every December. My mother would be out there, helping him, reminding him that he shouldn't curse in front of his daughter." Sam laughed softly. "But once they were up, he'd hoist me onto his shoulders and take me outside, even if I was already in my pajamas, to see them. And that's when I got to make a wish."

"A wish?"

"Yep. The first time the lights are turned on, my father said, was the most magical time, and he told me it was like birthday candles. Make a wish for Christmas and it would come true. I was a kid, so I was always wishing for a toy." Sam's smile faltered. "If I'd known…I would have wished for something else."

"Known what?"

"Known I wouldn't have had that many Christmases with him." She let out a breath, which became a cloud, framing her face in a soft mist. "I wish they were still alive."

"I'm sorry." And he was, because he knew her feelings.

She shrugged, as if she was over the loss, but Flynn saw a glistening in her eyes. "It's okay. My grandparents were there, and they were wonderful. The best substitute I could have asked for. What about your family? Did they hang lights every year? And curse their way through the process?"

"No."

They paused at a stop sign, even though there was no traffic. Sam turned to look at him, clearly surprised by his single-word answer. Flynn stepped off the curb and continued the walk.

"Did you live in an apartment? Is that why you didn't hang lights?"

What was with this woman? She was like a terrier with a new bone. She refused to give up on a topic. "No, that wasn't it. I just didn't celebrate Christmas much as a kid."

Sam halted on the sidewalk. "Really? Why?"

Flynn scowled. "I thought we were taking a walk. Not writing my biography."

The winter wind slithered between them, building an icy wall faster than a colony of ants could invade a picnic. Sam's hand slipped out of his and she stepped to the left, not a noticeable difference, but enough to send a signal.

He'd stopped getting personal, and she'd stopped connecting. He should be glad. He didn't want any kind of personal connection, anything that took him from the controlled path he'd always carefully maintained.

Then why did the bitter taste of disappointment pool in his gut?

"So, you said earlier you had some more questions to ask me," Sam said. "Did you remember what else you needed to know?"

Now that the time was here, and Sam was looking at him, waiting for him to ask the questions he knew he should—the kind he'd asked a hundred times before—

Flynn hesitated.

"Let's not talk business tonight. Let's just enjoy the walk."

She laughed, the sound as refreshing as lemonade on a hot summer day. "The intrepid reporter, getting sentimental? Dare I think the Winterfest actually got to you?"

No. *She'd* gotten to him. Every time he should be thinking about his job, he thought about kissing her. Every time he thought he was focused, he got distracted. And right now, when he was supposed to be taking the actions that would put his career back on top, everything within him started to rebel. For a man like Flynn, who lived life on a leash, that could only mean trouble.

"We have time anyway. It turns out my car won't be ready for another day or two." He thumbed in the general direction of Earl's shop. "So it looks like I'm stuck here."

She let out another little laugh. "You make it sound like you've been sentenced to a chain gang."

"Nah. Just Alcatraz."

She pressed a hand to her chest. "Flynn MacGregor, did you just make another joke?"

He grinned. "Not on purpose."

Flynn didn't know how they had done it, but their path had taken them to the park where the Winterfest had been held. On purpose? By accident?

He paused at the entrance. The lighted displays—gingerbread men, snowmen, Christmas trees, teddy bears—had all been left on, layering the grounds with silent, twinkling enchantment. The people were gone, Santa and Mrs. Claus back at home, the stands and games shut up for the night. Only the reindeer remained, chomping on some hay in his pen. The blanket of night gave everything a spirit of magic, as if anything could happen, as if, on this night, wishes could come true.

What would he have given to have gone to

something like this as a kid? To have been able to bring Liam to Santa's Workshop, to let him sit on Santa's lap, and tell Santa what he wanted—

And even more, have Santa actually deliver what he and Liam really desired?

The one thing neither of them had ever had. The only gift ripped away, time after time.

A home. A family. A place he could depend on, knowing it would be there this December 25th and the next, and that there would be someone there who would hang the lights and string garland on the tree.

Flynn shook his head. Damn. He hadn't intended to think about those days. Ever.

He felt a soft hand on his back. "Flynn? Are you all right?"

Sam. Her voice so gentle it called to him like a salve.

Maybe it was the timing. The darkness, punctuated by the sparkling holiday lights. Or maybe it was something more. Flynn didn't pause long enough to question why, he just turned toward Samantha Barnett and gave in to the desire that wrapped between them as tight as a bow on a present, and kissed her again.

When Flynn's lips met hers, Sam nearly stumbled backward in surprise. Then a wave of desire rocked her, and she leaned into him, her mouth parting against his. Their tongues danced, their bodies pressed together, heat building in crashing waves, even through the thick fabric of her winter coat.

His fingers tangled in her hair and her hood fell down, but she didn't feel the bite of winter, only the whoosh of desire as Flynn gently tugged her even closer.

Had she ever felt this treasured? Like she was the only woman in the world? The most special gift he had ever held? When he released her, disappointment slid all the way to her toes.

"We keep doing that," he said. "And we probably shouldn't."

"Yeah." Though right now, Sam couldn't think of a single reason why. "Not that I'm complaining," she added.

"I'm not complaining, either," he said. "And even though I know I shouldn't, because it shoots my reporter's objectivity all to hell, I couldn't resist." He caught a tendril of her hair and let it slip slowly through his grasp. "You are a very desirable woman."

"Oh, yeah, I'm a totally hot beauty right now." Sam ran a hand down her puffy jacket and let out a laugh. "I mean, I'm a walking marshmallow in this coat and even without it, I'm no skinny-minny, not to mention I—"

He put a finger to her lips. "You're beautiful,

just the way you are. Skinny doesn't automatically mean gorgeous. Nor was it your jacket that attracted me to you."

A shiver of pleasure ran down her spine. She hadn't been fishing for a compliment, but the words sent her heart singing. "Good, because if you were turned on by this thing, I'd be worried about you." She let out a laugh, but still it shook at the end. Flynn MacGregor had unnerved her, without a doubt.

"Do you find it that hard to believe that I'd be attracted to you?"

Sam broke away from Flynn and crossed to one of the displays, silent and immobile, but still lit, giving the town an all-night Christmas picture. She ran a hand down the lighted gingerbread mother, then up and over the circular heads of the little gingerbread children, all of them plump and happy in their wooden splendor.

"No..." But her voice trailed off, into the cold. Because she did. Flynn, the charming city man, who had surely dated women miles away from Sam, finding her attractive, seemed so unbelievable, yet very, very heady.

Silence held them in its uncomfortable grip for a long time, then Flynn came up behind her. "Who broke your heart, Samantha?"

"Is this on the record?" she asked, without turning around.

"Do you think that little of me, that I'd actually put your personal life into the story?"

She pivoted. "Would you, if you thought it would add more depth? Get you on the cover?"

He hesitated for only a fraction of a second, but it was enough to give her the answer she needed. Had any of this been real? Had he wanted her for her? Or for the story?

She needed to remember the truth. Behind every move Flynn MacGregor made, was an ulterior motive.

Sam's heart shattered in that instant. And even as Flynn said "no," Sam was already heading out of the park and back home.

Alone in the cold.

CHAPTER ELEVEN

THE MAN WAS LIKE A VIRUS.

Okay, maybe not a virus, but Flynn MacGregor had a tendency to be everywhere. Just when Sam thought she'd have a moment to breathe without him, he showed up, and disconcerted her all over again.

Heck, she'd been disconcerted ever since that kiss last night, not to mention the one before that, and all the times she'd thought about kissing him in between. She'd gone home, gone to bed, then tossed and turned for an hour, alternately berating herself for getting swept up in the moment and reliving the way his lips had moved against hers. The way he had awakened something inside of her that she'd thought didn't even exist.

The way he'd made her feel not just pretty, but beautiful. And then undone it all with the way he'd hesitated in his answer to her question.

He'd been at Joyful Creations first thing in the

morning, which had surprised her, considering the way they'd ended things last night—or rather the way she had ended the evening. She half expected him to get out his notepad and start asking questions, but instead he'd come into the kitchen and simply kept her company for the last few minutes.

Which had set her off-kilter, made her lose her concentration more than once.

What *did* he want?

"Uh, Sam, I'm not here to tell you how to do your job, but aren't you supposed to crack the eggs *before* you add them to the batter?" Flynn asked.

Sam looked down at the bowl, where three eggs sat, mocking her distractedness with their white oval shells. "Oh. Yeah." Her face flushed.

She fished the eggs out and cracked the shells against the edge, then turned on the professional-sized mixer, several times larger than one used in a regular kitchen. Instead of watching Flynn, she watched the dough turn and consume the yellow yolks.

"Why are you working today?" he asked. "It's Christmas Eve. How busy could you possibly be the day before Christmas?"

She turned off the mixer and reached for the sugar, measuring it into a large cup and pouring the crystals into the wide metal bowl. "You'd be surprised how many people have parties and need last-minute desserts. Or want Danishes for Christmas morning breakfast. It'll be busy in here. Though I do close early." She turned on the mixer and began incorporating the ingredients. "Technically, today's supposed to be my day off, but—" She shrugged, as if what he thought didn't matter. Sam turned away, feigning the study of a recipe in a book, before she started measuring her dry ingredients into a second bowl. She already knew the recipe by heart, but used the book as a way to avoid Flynn.

She'd do well to remember their roles. She was the story. He was the reporter. Getting any more personal with him than she already had would be a mistake.

If she did, she might end up spilling her personal beans, and he'd use her grandmother's story to throw in some human interest angle for his story about the bakery, making it national news, which would spread Grandma Joy's personal info all over Riverbend. She'd seen it happen too many times to other people—they became news charity cases. Sam refused to become another headline on Flynn's wall.

Flynn MacGregor would be gone in a day, two at most. She could keep her secrets safe that long. Protect her grandmother's privacy. She didn't want people knowing what had happened, realizing that Joy had lost the very memories that had once made her such a treasured part of this town.

That wouldn't do Joy or the people who loved her any good. All it would end up doing was creating a stirring of sympathy and a rush to "do something," when really, nothing could be done.

Flynn leaned against the doorjamb, his arms crossed over his chest. "Bet you haven't taken a Christmas Eve off, in…"

Sam began dropping teaspoonfuls of cookie dough onto cookie sheets. "About as long as you haven't."

"Touché." He moved closer to her. "Then why not take the day off?"

She paused in making cookies and studied him. "Are you suggesting we play hooky?"

"Exactly."

"But that would be…crazy. I never do that."

"Me neither."

She stared at him, stunned by the thought. All these years, heck, most of her life, she'd been working here full-time—more than full-time—and she couldn't even imagine the thought of leaving here for no good reason other than because she felt like it, and here she was thinking of doing exactly that for the second time in two days. "What would we do all day?"

Flynn cleared his throat. "Well, seeing as I have two choices—hanging out at Betsy's and listening to her struggle through Christmas carols or go to Earl's garage and hear his long-winded stories—both options painful in their own aural way," he said, wincing, "I thought I'd see if you…"

"What?" she asked when he didn't finish.

"Nothing. It's a crazy idea."

She tapped her lips, suddenly feeling game. It took her a second, but she put together the elements before her—guy, day of the year—and came up with what he'd been about to say. "Let me guess. You haven't bought a single Christmas present yet and wondered if I'd go shopping with you."

He shrugged. "Yeah."

Spending the day alone with Flynn would be a bad idea. She had enough work to do to keep her busy for a week, and he—

Well, he had this way of disrupting her equilibrium every time he entered a room. Sam prided herself on never letting those kinds of things happen. She was a levelheaded, practical businesswoman who made smart, well-thought-out decisions. Who put the right decision ahead of her personal temptations.

And Flynn could be dangerous if she let him get too close, a threat to everything she had worked so hard to build.

Yet, as she looked at his face, she saw a

flicker—so brief it could have been a trick of the light—of vulnerability and her heart went out to him. Then the look was gone, and he was back to his stalwart, standoffish self.

Was it just because they had shared a kiss? Or was it because she thought, just for a moment, that she had seen a kindred spirit in him? The man who'd left the Winterfest, unable to stay around the Christmas celebration, the man who she'd noticed appreciating the lights last night even if he wouldn't admit enjoying the twinkles, the same man who could barely talk about his own family?

Could it be that there was far more to Flynn MacGregor than met the eye? And maybe she had misjudged him?

She thought of the few hints of his life that he had given her, the way he seemed to avoid Christmas like most people avoided friends with the flu, and wondered whether he, like her, had reasons behind it all.

"You need a day off, more than anybody I know," he said, interrupting her thoughts. "And I need to shop. Since you're not very good at taking time off, and I really stink at shopping, the only solution is to work together. I don't know about you, but I could use a break." He took a step closer. "What do you say, Sam?"

"I have cookies to—"

"There will always be cookies to bake." Flynn took another step closer. "Come on, take the day off. For no reason, other than you just want to."

"And help you shop."

Flynn moved a little closer still, his hand inches from hers, triggering the memory of his kiss. "Something like that."

She knew she should say no. Knew she should stay right here, running the shop, baking cookies, filling orders. Except she didn't want to.

The craving for normalcy rose inside Sam, fast and fierce, tempered by guilt that she should stay. But the yearning for a life outside this bakery, doing ordinary things like shopping and dating, overpowered her, and she found herself tugging the apron off and tossing it onto the counter.

"Well, to be honest," Sam said, as everything inside her rebelled against the idea of working one more minute, "I haven't finished all my shopping yet, either."

"Let me guess. Too busy working to get to the store?"

"Something like that," she said, repeating his words. She didn't tell him that Christmas had lost its sparkle a long time ago. When her grandmother started forgetting holidays, when every day at the Heritage Nursing Home ran in Joy's head one after another, like an endless stream of Tuesdays. Without a husband, or a family, Sam just didn't have the desire to shop and celebrate like she used to. She still put up the tree, and made the attempt, but it wasn't the same.

"Yeah, me, too," Flynn said.

But as the two of them cleaned up the kitchen, then left the little shop, while Aunt Ginny offered—with a knowing wink—to stay behind with the temporary workers and cover the day's customers, Sam began to worry that she'd just made a huge mistake.

What had he been thinking?

Flynn could name on one hand the number of people he needed to shop for. Mimi. Liam. Who probably wouldn't even open the gift anyway. Maybe his editor. Most years, Flynn just dropped off a fruit basket for the office, if he even thought of that.

Hey, he was a guy. Gift-giving wasn't exactly his forte.

He knew why he'd proposed the shopping trip. It hadn't been about escaping Betsy's piano playing. Or Earl's stories. He'd been looking for something to fill the day, the hours until his car was fixed, and spending that time with Sam had seemed like a good idea when he'd been standing in the back of her little shop, wrapped in the scent of cookies. The deep green of her eyes.

He could tell himself it was because he still

wanted to get to the heart of his story, to find out about her grandmother. To finish those final pieces of his article.

But that wasn't it at all.

He wanted to be with her, craved her presence, in a way he'd never craved anything before. She represented all the things he hadn't thought existed. Small towns, with families where parents raised their children, made a life based on love and commitment.

The kind of life he'd dreamed of, and never imagined he could have. For just a little while longer, before he had to go back to real life, he'd hold on to that dream.

Now, they wandered the aisles of a cramped antiques shop, looking at trinkets he had no use for and furniture he'd never bring to his apartment, not that he was home enough to even use the furniture he already had. He picked up a white dish that looked like it had beads imbedded in the edge, then set it down again. Fingered the fringe on the edge of a lamp so gaudy, he couldn't even imagine what sight-challenged artist had designed it in the first place—or why.

"Finding anything?" Sam asked. Her arms were laden with purchases. A wide painted bowl, a leather-bound book, a hand-cut glass vase and an intricate wrought-iron wine rack. Everything she'd picked out looked tasteful and perfect, the kinds of things he could imagine in his own home, if he ever bought a house.

"Nope."

A smile curved across her face. "You're totally out of your league, aren't you?"

"Well…" He looked around the shop. "Yeah."

"And I bet this isn't exactly your kind of place, is it?"

"Not quite. I was thinking something more… fancy. Maybe a jewelry shop?" A bracelet or some earrings, he knew would make Mimi happy. Other than that, he had no idea which way her tastes ran.

It occurred to him that he had probably spent more time inside Sam's bakery than he had inside Mimi's apartment. He'd have an easier time buying Sam a home decoration than his own girl-friend, if that was even the label he could put on Mimi.

Sam thought about that for a second. "I know where we can go. Let me just purchase these. Then we can head down to Indianapolis. There's civilization there. Meaning a mall." She gave him a grin.

"Civilization." Flynn drew in a deep breath, as if he could suck up the city from here. "That's the one thing I'd pay about anything to have."

He should have been excited, but for some reason, the expected lilt of anticipation didn't rise in his chest. Even the knowledge that his car would be ready tomorrow—meaning he could leave—didn't excite him like it should.

He attributed it to a lack of sleep, or too many renditions of "Jingle Bells" ringing in his ears from Betsy's overactive piano fingers. Because he certainly hadn't started to like this town. There was *no way* Riverbend was beginning to grow on him.

He'd feel better when he got to the city. Away from this overdone home of all things Christmas. Back to the cold, impersonal world he knew.

Flynn took several of the items from Sam's arms, earning a surprised thank-you, and a few minutes later, she had paid and they were inside her Jeep, on their way out of town. The snow had started up again, falling in thick, heavy flakes. "Does it ever stop snowing around here?"

"Welcome to the Midwest. Although this month, we are getting a record amount of snow, so you're getting a treat." She shot him a smile. "You're from the East Coast. Don't you get a lot of snow, too?"

"I live in the city. I guess I don't notice as much."

"This storm is supposed to stop tomorrow. And we should be fine. I have four-wheel drive on the Jeep. If not—" Sam looked over at him "—are you up for an adventure?"

Flynn glanced down at his dress shoes and cashmere coat. "I'm not exactly prepared for much beyond a dinner party."

"Well, then, Flynn MacGregor," she said with that laugh in her voice that rang as easily as church bells, "you better hope nothing goes wrong on our expedition."

Sam should have kept her mouth shut.

Twenty miles outside of town, the Jeep suddenly got hard to steer. Sam attributed the stubborn wheel to the icy roads, until she saw steam coming from the hood. She pulled over, wrestling with the steering wheel to get the Jeep to come to a stop at the side of the road.

"Overheated?" Flynn asked.

"Maybe. I have no idea what's wrong. Are you handy with cars?"

"Are you kidding me? If I was, I would have fixed my own and been gone long before now."

Steam curled in twin vicious clouds from under the hood, spreading outward in a mysterious burst that spelled certain doom for the engine. Sam sighed. "Well. That doesn't look good."

"Let me take a look under the hood."

"I thought you said you weren't good with cars."

"I'm not, but considering we have zero options

here, I figure I can't make it any worse." He gestured toward the windshield. "Pop the hood. Maybe I'll get some mechanical vibes from the engine."

Sam pulled the latch for the Jeep's hood, then waited inside while Flynn got out and went around to the front of the car. When the worst of the steam had cleared, Flynn leaned in to look at the engine. One minute passed. Two. She heard him tinker with something.

Finally, Sam climbed out of the Jeep and joined him at the front of the SUV. "Did you find anything?"

"Radiator fluid is fine. But your oil is low." He held up a dipstick.

Furious gusts of wind blew into Sam and Flynn, and snow drifts skittered across the highway in white sheets. Sam shivered and raised her voice over the howling storm. "I don't think that's the problem. Do you?"

"No." Flynn slid the long skinny stick back into place, then leaned farther inside. Another chilly thirty seconds passed. "I'm no expert, but I'd say *that's* your problem." He pointed into the dark depths of the engine.

"I don't see anything."

"Right there."

Sam moved over, until her shoulder brushed against his, and despite the cold and the bulky layers of her coat, a jolt of electricity ran through her. For a second, she forgot about the engine. Awareness of the man beside her slammed into Sam like a tidal wave.

"Do you see the problem?"

Oh, yes. She did. All six foot two of him.

"It's right there," Flynn said.

Get a grip, Sam.

They were stuck in the middle of nowhere, with a blizzard bearing down on them. This was not the time to go off on a hot man tangent, not when she had a major hot car problem.

"Uh, is it that what you're talking about?" Sam pointed at a frayed belt buried deep in the engine.

"Yep. Like I said, I'm no mechanic, but even I know a broken belt is a problem. Whichever belt this is, it's an important one."

The snow continued to fall, building up so fast, the engine was already covered with a fluffy white blanket. Flynn ran a hand over his hair, mussing the straight lines, and sending a spray of flakes to the ground. "We need to get out of the storm."

They hurried back inside the Jeep. Sam shuddered and rubbed her hands up and down her arms. "It's getting cold out there."

"And we can't stay in the car. It's not running and it won't hold whatever heat it has for very long." Flynn flipped out his cell phone, held it up toward the angry gray sky, then let out a curse. "Is there anywhere around here that has a cell tower?"

Sam gave him a smile. "We were driving *toward* civilization, if that helps."

"Well, we're going to need something approaching civilization or we'll become Popsicles pretty soon."

Sam looked out the window. The blizzard had picked up steam, and no cars were on the road. She should have checked the weather forecast before deciding on this impromptu shopping trip. Clearly, it had been a bad idea. And now, they were stranded, with nowhere to go.

Then, a little way down the road, she spied a familiar orange sign, tacked to a light pole. Serendipity, or a miracle, Sam didn't question which it was.

"My father used to hunt in this area when I was a little girl," Sam said. "I never went with him, but I know he and his friends used to stay overnight sometimes. That means there must be a hunters' cabin out here somewhere."

Flynn cupped a hand over his eyes and peered out into the white. "That's the problem. It's somewhere."

"It's better than staying here and freezing to death."

"True."

"Riverbend is twenty miles behind us. The next town is thirty miles south. Either we find the cabin or hope someone else was stupid enough not to check the weather before getting on the road."

"What are the chances of that?" Flynn asked. He took one more look down the road, in both directions. Empty, as far as the eye could see, visibility closing to almost nothing. "Well, you told me to be up for an adventure. I guess this is it."

CHAPTER TWELVE

IT TOOK THEM CLOSE to an hour to find the rustic cabin, nestled deep in the woods off the highway. By that time, Flynn's shoes were ruined, and the snow had soaked through his gabardine pants, all the way to his knees. His coat, which had seemed warm enough for the season when he bought it, turned out to be little protection against the biting winter wind.

But then again, when he'd bought the cashmere coat, it hadn't been with the intention of traipsing through the woods, searching for a hunters' cabin.

Sam was better prepared for the weather, in her thick parka and boots. Still, her face was red and she looked ready to collapse by the time they spied the small wood structure.

"Finally," Sam said, the word escaping with a cloud of breath. She hurried forward, pumping her arms to help her navigate the deep snow. "I can feel the heat already."

He grabbed her sleeve. "Wait. We should gather some dry wood so we can start a fire."

Sam drew up short. "Of course. I can't believe I didn't think of that. Maybe there will be some over there—"

"No. You go inside and I'll get the wood." He gestured toward the cabin.

She gave him a dubious look. "You are hardly dressed to go gallivanting through the forest looking for firewood."

"I'm not letting you go gallivanting through the forest, either," Flynn said as they continued through the woods, stopping when they reached the stoop of the cabin—if the few slats of wood under a one-foot overhang could even be called a stoop.

"Oh, I get it. This is you playing the gentleman. I'm supposed to wait inside, because I'm the girl, is that it?"

"Well…yeah."

"I can take care of myself."

"I have no doubt that you can. And that I can take care of you, too." This woman could sure be stubborn when she wanted to be. It was probably what made her such a good business owner, what had gotten her through those difficult years when she was young, but damn it, he wasn't going to let her go running off in the woods alone.

Sam laughed. "You, take care of me? I

probably have more survival skills in my left foot than you have in your—"

He put a finger to her lips, and when he did, he became acutely aware that they were alone in the woods. That it had been twelve hours since he'd kissed her. And how very much he wanted to kiss her again. "You don't know me as well as you think you do. So why don't you go inside, and let me do this?"

She considered him for a long moment, then shrugged concession. "Do you want my boots?"

He grinned. "I think your feet are just a bit smaller than mine."

"All the more reason why I—"

"I'm not arguing this." He'd take care of her whether she liked it or not, not out of some macho need to be the guy, but because she was the kind of woman who deserved to have a man take care of her—and the first woman to tell him she didn't. Flynn reached forward and pulled open the cabin door. The outside light spilled into the cabin, illuminating part of the interior. "Let's go inside, and I'll light a candle or something for you, then I can go looking for firewood."

Sam started to laugh.

"What's so funny?"

"Apparently, you don't have to go far, Superman." She pointed inside the small, musty building. Against the wall, a pile of wood had been stacked in a pyramid. "But at least I know you would have taken care of me, if I needed you to."

He would have, even if he'd had to go back into the woods barefoot, but he didn't say that. She might be great at the helm of her bakery, but out here, he knew what to do.

"Well, that's a start. I'll get a fire going, then load us up, in case we're stuck here for a while." Flynn stomped the snow off his shoes, then crossed to the fireplace. He rubbed his hands together to bring some feeling back into his fingers, then laid the kindling in the cold cavern. Flynn found a box of matches on the mantel, and a few moments later had a tiny flame licking at the edges of the small sticks.

He kept his back to Sam, feeding the flame, one piece of wood at a time. It was far easier to do that than to consider the fire brewing behind him.

One he hadn't counted on when he'd first arrived in Riverbend. One he hadn't counted on at all.

It wasn't the flames that had Sam amazed so much as how fast Flynn MacGregor coaxed them from the wood. Of all the people she would have listed as least likely to be able to build a fire, he would have topped the list. And yet, here he was, stoking the fire and building it gradually, like he'd been a Boy Scout all his life.

Flynn MacGregor. The same man who'd walked into Riverbend wearing expensive leather shoes and a cashmere coat. The one who'd hated small-town life, and seemed like he'd never been more than five minutes outside of a city. And here he was, bringing in wood from the forest, laying it by the fire to dry, then expertly tending to the fireplace, warming the tiny cabin so fast, Sam could hardly remember being cold.

Well, it was Christmas. The season of miracles, after all.

The cabin was small, about a fifteen foot square, and not exactly five-star accommodations. Rough pine walls had been nailed together enough to block the weather, but not so well that they kept out all drafts. There was no insulation, no drywall. Nothing fancy that would make anyone mistake this hunting cabin for anything more than a temporary stopping place. A kitchen table and two chairs sat on one end of the single-room cabin, and a threadbare cushion covered a log-framed couch on the other. Against the far wall, a set of bunk beds with plastic mattresses, apparently made for sleeping bags instead of fine linens, waited for weary hunters. In the kitchen, a shelf of canned goods sat beside two pots and a couple of spoons. Sam suspected she wouldn't find much more than a few forks and knives in the single drawer beside a rudimentary dry sink.

As Flynn worked on the fire, she grabbed a few jarred candles from the shelf, then lit them and set them around the room. She also found a hurricane lamp and after a lot of fiddling, got it to light.

Okay, so the whole atmosphere was oddly romantic, but Sam ignored the flickering flames, the soft glow. They were here to get out of the storm. A temporary place to get warm. Soon, the storm would stop and they could make a plan.

When Flynn was done, he swung the sofa around to face the fire. A cozy sitting place, just for the two of them. "It's not the Ritz, but it should do until the storm blows over."

"It's great. Thank you."

"You're welcome."

They were quiet, the only sound in the room coming from the crackling of the logs and the occasional soft thud of a snow chunk falling from the roof. For the first time, Sam became aware that they were alone. Totally alone.

And as much as she hoped otherwise, it could be hours. Many, many hours, until the storm ended and she could get a tow truck to pick up the Jeep. That meant they'd be stuck here, for an indefinite period of time.

"You should come over here and get warm." Flynn took off his damp coat and draped it over the arm of the sofa. "And take off whatever is wet, so you don't get sick."

"I'm fine." Way over here. Bundled up. Not so tempted to kiss him then.

Flynn crossed to her and placed a palm against her cheek. The touch warmed her, not just because of body heat, but because every time Flynn MacGregor touched her, he seemed to set off some kind of instant thermal jump inside her. "You're freezing. Come on, sit by the fire. And don't argue with me."

Sam's protests were cut off by Flynn taking her hand and leading her over to the sofa. She stood there, her palms outstretched to greet the heat emanating in waves, still a human marshmallow, until Flynn slipped between her and the fire and began to unzip her coat. "What are you doing?"

"Your coat is soaked. I know it's waterproof, but that doesn't mean it's completely impervious to snow." He slipped his hands under the fabric and over her shoulders, sliding the heavy fabric off. His gaze caught hers, and heat rose in her chest. Desire quivered in her gut, then coiled tight against her nerves. Her breath caught, held. Flynn's thumbs ran over her collarbone, sending a tingle down her spine.

His gaze captured hers. A second passed. Another.

"What are we doing here?" The words whispered out of her.

"Getting out of the storm."

"Is that what we're really doing?"

Flynn released her and stepped away, bending to retrieve her coat from the floor. "Yes. That's all."

Sam moved closer to the fire, running her arms up and down her sleeves, warding off a chill she didn't feel. Behind her, Flynn pulled one of the kitchen chairs closer to the flames, and draped her jacket over the back, leaving it to dry in the heat. She expected him to join her at the fire, but he paused for a long second behind her, then she heard his footsteps recede.

A moment later, he was in the kitchen, going through the canned goods, pulling one after another off the shelves until finding whatever he was looking for.

Sam remained where she was, trying to calm the turbulent waters in her gut. What was it with this man? Was it just that he was a stranger? A sexy city guy who offered something new and different? Or had she simply been cooped up with that mixer too long?

Every time she was near him, she forgot the hundreds of reasons she shouldn't get involved with him. Most of all, she forgot reason number one. When Flynn drew near, when his gaze captured hers, she lost track of her goals—with the business, this article, her future, her family—and that was reason enough not to get distracted by him.

Flynn brushed past her, a pot in one hand, and a long-handled contraption in the other. He set up the handled thing near the fire, then attached the pot, swinging it out and over the flames. They licked eagerly at the bottom of the pan, heating whatever was in there as easily as they had Sam.

She watched him cook, stunned, speechless. He seemed to know exactly what he was doing, because a few minutes later, he swung the pot back, took it off the handle and brought it back to the kitchen.

Well. She hadn't expected that. Flynn *cooking?*

"Spaghetti surprise," Flynn said, returning and holding a plate out to Sam.

She bit back a laugh at the sight of canned spaghetti topped with crushed saltines. "You are very inventive, Mr. MacGregor. I had no idea you could do all this, or come up with a recipe for dinner, based on what was in there."

"Hey, I had to be inventive when I was—" He cut off the sentence. "There wasn't much to work with in the kitchen."

What had he been about to say? What personal tidbits was he leaving out? Every time she got close, he seemed to shut the door on himself. Because he didn't want her to get to know him? Or because there were things about himself that he didn't want to share?

She had no right to criticize him, Sam realized. She'd yet to tell him the truth about her grandmother. Heck, she'd yet to tell the town the truth about her grandmother, the same customers who patronized Joyful Creations every day, and asked about Joy just as often.

Sam thanked him, for the food, but deep down inside, she was even more grateful for the diversion.

They took seats on opposite ends of the sofa and began to eat. The odd dish turned out to be far more appetizing than it had looked. "Where did you learn this particular recipe?"

Flynn picked at his dish, but didn't take another bite. He let out a long breath, then put his plate down on his knee. He hesitated, as if warring with himself about the answer, before finally speaking. "Foster care."

"Foster care? You were in foster care?" Again, another major surprise. Not something she would have associated with him.

At all.

"Let's just say not all the places I lived were

the best, so I learned how to take care of myself. And sometimes, I was taking care of my brother, too."

"Sometimes?"

"Not every foster family wanted the two-for-one deal."

The words slammed into Sam. She may have lost her parents when she was young—far too young, she'd always thought—but she had grown up in a happy, two-parent home, first with her parents and then later with Grandma Joy and Grandpa Neil. She'd always had grandparents around, a town she'd known all her life, lots of people who loved her. Stability.

She'd never had to live with strangers. Never had to concoct spaghetti surprise.

Sam laid a hand on his arm. "I'm so sorry, Flynn."

He shrugged. "I turned out okay. And I learned some cooking skills."

At what price? Sam looked at Flynn with new eyes. Knowing his past, or at least the little he had shared so far, explained so much. The way he'd reacted to Riverbend. The way he held himself back from people, didn't engage, didn't connect. All along, she'd faulted him, thinking he was disagreeable, only after the story, when he'd simply been someone who probably hadn't had a chance to find a home. To find people to connect with.

Sympathy rode through her in a wave, and she made a vow.

A vow to give Flynn MacGregor the best darn Christmas ever. Assuming, that was, that he let her. And they ever got out of this cabin and the storm.

"What happened to your parents?" she asked.

He made a face, as if he didn't want to talk about the subject, then let out a long breath. "I've never talked to anyone, besides Liam, about my childhood."

"Oh." She didn't know if that meant he didn't want her to ask, or if he meant the opposite. She simply waited, allowing Flynn to call whatever shots he wanted.

"It's not an easy topic for me." He picked at his food, but didn't eat, as if the twist of noodles on his plate held some answers she couldn't see. Before them, a log split, the fissure hissing and spitting sparks. "My mother was…not the most responsible person on the planet. She never knew who my father was. Mine or Liam's."

Again, Sam reached out a hand to Flynn, laying her palm gently on his wrist. She was here, and she would listen. That, she suspected, was what he needed most right this second.

"She was an addict. Nothing too heavy when I was born, but by the time Liam came along, she was doing cocaine. Nothing could get her to stop, not even getting pregnant. They tested him for drugs in his system at birth, and that was it. We were yanked out of the house, and even though she made a stab at getting clean a few times, it never stuck. So we bounced around the foster care system all our lives. She overdosed before we were in high school."

Sam gasped. "Oh, Flynn, that's awful. I can't even imagine."

"Don't. Because whatever picture you come up with, it's probably not half as bad as the reality. I'm not saying all foster care is terrible, because there are a lot of good foster families out there, but Liam and I never seemed to hit the family lottery. We were…" He shrugged. "Difficult."

"You were traumatized."

"Yeah, well, in those days, that wasn't what they called it."

Her heart broke for him, and even though she knew it was impossible, Sam wished she could go back in time, and make up for all those years. Take away all the rejections, the shuffling from place to place. Somehow give Flynn and his brother the home they'd never had. "And Liam? Did he do okay?"

A smile filled Flynn's face. Clearly, he loved his brother. "He's at Purdue University, going for a master's in engineering. He's smart as hell. And thank God, he's turned out just fine."

"Because you were there for him."

"Not enough," Flynn said quietly. "Not enough."

She heard the guilt in his voice. That was an emotion she understood, too well. "Are you still planning on seeing him before you go back to Boston?"

Flynn rose and grabbed a log, tossing it onto the fire. He watched the flames curl around the wood, accepting it and devouring the bark, then eating into the wood. "No."

"Why not?"

"We lost touch when he went away to college. It was always hard for Liam, and he was younger, so he didn't always understand. I tried my best..." Flynn rose, dusted his hands together. "I just tried my best."

"I'm sure you've done plenty, Flynn."

He shook his head. "I watched out for Liam when I could, but we weren't always together. That hurt him, more than me. It's made him...distant. It's like an old joke. You think I'm detached?" He looked up at her, his face no joke, but filled with the pain of separation, of losing the sole family member he had. "You should meet my brother."

"Oh, Flynn," Sam said, reaching for him where he stood, but he didn't want the comfort, not yet. It was as if he needed to say the words, get them out in one painful pass.

"Everything we went through was so much harder on him because he was younger. I can't take those years back. I can't undo the damage." Flynn ran a hand through his hair and sighed, the sound pouring from him like concrete. "All I can do is make it up to him the best way I know how. Keep taking care of him, but this time with dollars."

Guilt lined Flynn's face, and his shoulders sagged beneath a burden only he could feel. For a moment, she wanted to reach out, to tell him she shared that burden. That she felt that pain every time she brought her grandmother cookies, a new sweater or simply made sure the nurses and staff had her favorite blanket on her bed. Instead, Sam kept her secrets walled inside. "You pay for everything for him?"

Flynn shrugged. "Yeah. But he...won't talk to me."

"Maybe..." She paused. "Maybe he wants you, not the money."

"Maybe. Maybe not." Flynn returned to the sofa and picked up his plate again. "Fire's doing well, don't you think?"

"It is." The heat was so good, it was making her drowsy. Sam tucked her legs beneath her, and leaned closer to Flynn. She let the subject of his brother drop. She certainly didn't have a right to tell others how to handle their relationships with loved ones when she wasn't taking anyone's advice, either. "Who taught you to build a fire?"

"There was one house," Flynn said, stirring his food, "we stayed at for almost a year. The father there, he was into camping. Loved the outdoors. He took my brother and me a few times, and made sure we knew how to survive." Flynn scoffed, then his voice softened, going so quiet Sam had to strain to hear him. "Turned out, that was the one skill I'd need the most."

"What do you mean?"

Flynn rose, forcing her touch to drop away, and crossed to the kitchen, depositing his plate on the counter. "Considering how well you bake, I'm sure you're a hell of a cook, Sam. You probably would have done a better job than me."

The subject of his childhood was closed. He couldn't have made that any clearer if he'd hung up a sign. Sam could hardly blame him. She'd been hanging No Trespassing signs around her own heart for years.

But for the first time, she began to wonder if maybe the time had come to take a few of the signs down. And take a chance again.

CHAPTER THIRTEEN

WHAT HAD HE been thinking?

For five minutes there, Flynn had lost control. Had opened the door to a past he'd vowed never to visit. Not again. Instead of continuing the conversation, he melted some snow over the fire and used it to wash the dishes and put them back.

But that only killed a few minutes.

Long, potentially endless hours stretched before him. Alone with Samantha Barnett. A woman he told himself, over and over again, that he wouldn't get involved with. Wouldn't open himself up to, emotionally.

Except for those kisses. Yeah, there had been that. And the fact that he wanted to repeat those. Again and again. Wanted still to take her in his arms, even as he knew he shouldn't.

What he should really be doing, instead of spilling his guts over some lousy canned spaghetti, was getting the story his editor was paying him to find. Start probing *Sam* for answers instead of spitting out his own every five seconds like some crazy self-pity candy machine.

"Do you need some help?"

Sam's voice, soft as silk, over his shoulder. "No, I've got it."

"Listen, I didn't mean to intrude earlier. If you don't want to talk about your childhood, I understand."

"Like I said, it's not my favorite subject."

"Then how about we spend the rest of our time here doing something else?"

The invitation in her voice brought the roar of desire, one he'd barely been holding back, to life again. Flynn laid the last dish on the shelf and turned to her. "I don't think—"

And saw that Sam was holding a deck of cards. "I found these in one of the drawers. Are you up for some gin rummy?"

She'd meant card games. Not kissing. Not anything else.

He should have been grateful, but, damn it, he wasn't.

What did he want? Flynn crossed the room, following behind Sam's curvy figure, and knew, without a doubt what he wanted.

Everything.

He wanted to get the story, get out of Indiana, go back to Boston, keep his job, and—

Have this moment with Sam. To forget that he was Flynn MacGregor, a man who'd never known this kind of sweet simplicity, the kind that she believed in as devoutly as children believed in Santa Claus. To surrender to the same beliefs, and just…

Have a merry Christmas.

In the last few days, that Christmas spirit had started to rub off on him, as silly as the thought was. The possibility that Flynn, of all people, could have what Riverbend offered began to feel…real. It sounded so easy. But for Flynn, nothing had ever been that easy.

Still, he ended up at the kitchen table with Sam, who dealt the cards. He vaguely remembered how to play gin rummy, and fanned his cards in front of him.

"Flynn? Your turn. Lay down or discard."

"Oh, yeah. Sorry." He discarded an ace he'd really wanted to keep, which Sam promptly picked up and used to make her own triplet of aces, crowing with delight over the find. Three minutes later, Sam had trounced him at cards.

She leaned forward to collect his cards, getting ready to deal again. "Your mind's not in the game, MacGregor," she teased. "You keep playing like that and—"

Flynn leaned forward, cupped a hand around her neck, and kissed her again. The fire crackled softly, sending quiet waves of heat over them, but there was already plenty of heat brewing in the kitchen. Flynn's fingers tangled in Sam's blond mane, dancing up and down the tender skin of her neck, while his mouth captured the sweet taste of hers.

Her tongue darted into his mouth, dancing a slow, sensual tango, which only served to inflame the desire in his gut. Flynn groaned, sliding out of his chair to get closer. His hand drifted down, over her shoulder, along her arm, sliding around to cup her breast through the thick fabric of her sweater.

Sam arched against him, responding with a fervor that matched his own. She whispered his name into his mouth, and Flynn nearly came undone.

Had he ever known anyone this sexy? A woman who could make him fall apart with a kiss, the mere mention of his name?

Sam curved into him, her arms going around his back, holding him tight, as if she couldn't bring him close enough. His kiss deepened, wanting more of her, so much more than he could have.

Finally, reluctantly, he pulled back. "If we, ah—" he caught his breath "—don't stop, we'll probably end up finding ways to pass the time that we hadn't intended."

Sam's green gaze was steady on his, deep, still filled with desire. Against his chest, her heart hammered a matching beat. "And that would be bad."

"Very." Though he was having trouble thinking of very many reasons right now.

"Because…"

"We don't know each other very well."

"There is that."

He traced a finger down her cheek, along her jawline, fighting the growing desire to kiss her again, to taste that sweet skin. "And we should probably be thinking about ways of getting out of here."

Sam sighed. "Yeah, we probably should."

And he should be focusing on his job. On what was important. Kissing a woman he had no intention of staying with didn't even make the list.

So, he tried. He picked up the deck of cards, dealt them out again and tried to concentrate on the game.

And failed miserably.

A rock band drummed in Sam's head. Pounding, pounding, calling her name…

"Sam! You in there?"

She jerked awake, just in time to see Earl stumble into the cabin, along with a flurry of snow and a barking dog. Beside her, Flynn popped to his feet. The two of them had fallen asleep after playing cards, the heat of the fire and the exhaustion of the day finally catching up with them. "Earl?"

"You're alive! Well, thank the Lord in heaven. I thought sure I'd be finding myself two Popsicles in the woods." Earl brushed a load of snow off the top of his hat. The golden retriever started running around the cabin, sniffing every corner, his tail wagging, as if he'd just latched on to his own personal treasure trove.

"What are you doing here?" Flynn asked. He had already disentangled himself from Sam, and gotten off the sofa.

Had Earl seen them like that, lying in each other's arms? And how had they fallen asleep like that? Sam remembered sitting on the sofa, talking lazily with Flynn about when the storm might end…

And then nothing.

Earl stared at them like they were idiots. "Looking for you."

"How did you know we were here?" Sam said.

"Ol' Earl's not as dumb as he looks. Plus, your man here told Betsy he was going shopping. And you, Sam, told your Aunt Ginny you'd be back this afternoon. She called Betsy, looking for you, all worried that you weren't back yet. Me and Betsy, we were gettin' cozy—" Earl paused, cast a glance at the sofa, then cleared his throat

"—we were talking, just talking, and we put two and two together, and got thirty-one."

Earl had seen them. Great. He'd tell Betsy, and the next thing Sam knew, the whole town would be planning her wedding.

Flynn shook his head. "Two and two adds up to four, Earl."

Earl removed his cap and gave Flynn a grin. "Not when you and Sam are on highway thirty-one, it don't."

"Whatever math you're using," Sam said, crossing to give Earl a hug, "I'm glad you found us. We were worried we'd be stuck here forever."

Earl's face reddened, from collar to hairline. "Aww, it was nothing, Sam. Really." He stepped out of the embrace, twirling his cap in his hands.

The golden retriever, done with his search of the cabin, came bounding over to them, pausing by Sam for an ear-scratch, before heading to Flynn and jumping on him. Flynn looked surprised for a second, then patted the dog. In response, the golden retriever licked Flynn's face then jumped down again. Flynn swiped at his jaw. "What's the dog for?"

"That's Paulie Lennox's worthless mutt. Supposed to be good for tracking, but Gracie there, she didn't find nothin' but two black squirrels. If I'd had my shotgun, we'd all be having squirrel for dinner—"

Flynn blanched.

Earl chuckled and clapped him on the shoulder. "Just kidding there, city boy. I draw the line at animals that climb trees."

"We have that in common."

"See? Told you that you'd fit into this town." Earl plopped his hat back on his head. "Are you two about ready to leave? Or you thinking of moving in here? I gotta admit, it's mighty cozy here. Maybe this summer me and my Betsy…" He colored again. "Well. Time to go."

A flicker of sadness ran through Sam. She should be glad to be getting out of the cabin. Back home. Her Aunt Ginny was undoubtedly worried sick, and things at the bakery were probably insane without her there.

But as they doused the fire, tidied the cabin, and headed out the door, Sam couldn't help but feel a little regret that the small oasis she'd found with Flynn MacGregor had come to an end. They were going back to the real world.

And soon, he'd be going back to his.

"Good news," Earl said, while he drove them back to town, in a pickup truck that had been built long before Flynn had been born. "Your part came in while you were out traipsing through the woods."

"My part?"

"My goodness, boy, I think the snow has damaged your frontal lobe." Earl looked over at him. "For your car. I put it in and your car is running like a dream again. I told you ol' Earl would take care of you. Now you can hightail it out of town. And just in time for Christmas tomorrow."

Christmas.

He'd be heading back to Boston. To his apartment. Alone.

He should have been happy, but he was inexplicably disappointed. Irritated, even. Like he wished the part hadn't arrived. That his car would remain on Earl's lift for a couple more days. What was up with that?

Mimi would have already flown to Paris, or Monte Carlo, or wherever it was that she had chosen to spend her holiday this year. Mimi didn't do holidays—except New Year's Eve, which was an occasion to host a social event, and get noticed by people in the business. Flynn tended to avoid Mimi's parties, the crush of strangers, because they were always more of a networking tool than a celebration.

And Liam? Liam was probably with his friends, or a girlfriend. Flynn hadn't talked to his brother in so long, he wasn't quite sure. The chances of Liam still being on campus tomorrow were about zero.

Most years, Flynn didn't mind that his Christmases were anything but conventional. He couldn't remember the last time he'd had anything even remotely resembling a traditional December 25th.

In fact, most years, Flynn *preferred* to be alone on holidays. It gave him time to catch up, to clear out his desk, go through the backlog of e-mails, and most of all—

Pretend he didn't care that there was no one's house to drive to for a turkey dinner and a slew of presents to open. That it didn't matter that Liam hadn't returned his calls. Or that he hadn't called Liam, either. Because for a while there, the brothers had lost touch and stopped relying on each other because it was easier than connecting and being torn apart again and again.

It was this town. And most of all, Samantha Barnett. The two of them had gotten him dreaming of something he'd never really had— a real Christmas.

He fished his cell phone out of his pocket and flipped it open. He scrolled through the list of contacts until he got to Liam's name. The four letters stared back at him, simple and plain.

"Oh, look," Sam said from her position in the backseat. "You finally have a signal. If there's anyone you want to call." Her gaze met his in the rearview mirror. "Tomorrow's Christmas, Flynn."

He had a signal. He could make a call, if he needed to, as Sam had said. The phone weighed heavy against his palm. He ran his thumb over the send button, but didn't press the green circle.

"Gas station coming up in a few miles," Earl said. "I need to stop and fill the ol' bucket up."

"Great," Sam said. "I could really use a cup of coffee. Flynn? How about you?"

"Huh?"

"Coffee?"

"Yeah. That sounds like a good idea."

But when they finally did pull over, Earl got out to pump gas, and instead of staying behind to make a call, Flynn offered to head inside to get the coffee, leaving his phone on the dashboard.

CHAPTER FOURTEEN

SAM WAS FORCED to go straight home. Earl refused to drop her off at the bakery. He told her in no uncertain terms that it was Christmas Eve and no fool in her right mind worked the night before Christmas. "And you, my dear Sam, are no fool," Earl said. "You have yourself a merry Christmas. I'll get your Jeep on December twenty-sixth, and fix it up, good as new."

"Thanks, Earl." Sam left the truck, and traipsed up her stairs, Flynn behind her. She unlocked the door, then paused. "Do you want to come in for a while?"

Earl tooted his horn, then pulled away, tossing Sam a grin and a wave as he did. "Looks like my ride has left me," Flynn said.

"Everyone in this town is a matchmaker," Sam muttered.

"What?"

"Nothing."

Flynn cast a glance at the dark sky. "I should probably get back to Betsy's. Finish my article, get packed…" His voice trailed off. He toed at the porch. "Earl's got my car ready, so I can get on the road."

"It's Christmas Eve, Flynn. Surely you aren't thinking of driving home tonight."

Flynn flicked out his wrist and checked his watch. "It's a fourteen-, or fifteen-hour drive back to Boston. The longer I stay here, the longer it is 'til I get my article turned in. I could take a chance on getting it e-mailed from here, but the Internet connection is too spotty. So I should—"

"Should what? Hurry home for a Christmas that's no Christmas at all?" She leaned against the open door and faced him. No way was she going to let him go without making a good attempt to get this man to enjoy the holiday. Not after what he'd told her back in the cabin. He, of everyone she knew, deserved more than that. "What's waiting for you back in Boston? An empty apartment? A half a bottle of wine in a refrigerator filled with take-out boxes?"

"I doubt my fridge is filled with anything. I don't eat at home often enough to even leave the leftovers in there."

"Exactly my point."

He thumbed in the direction behind him. "My car is—"

"Still going to be ready the day after Christmas. You should stay here. And have a Christmas, a real one, for once. Look at this town. It's Christmas personified. Where else are you going to find a bed-and-breakfast owner wearing jingle bells, for Pete's sake?"

He quirked a grin at her. "Are you trying to convince me to stay?"

"I'm offering you the deal of the year. A holiday you won't forget." She'd do whatever it took tomorrow—bake a ham, light the candles, sing the carols—if it would give Flynn the Christmas she suspected he had yet to have.

He shook his head, the slight smile still playing at his lips, as if he could tell he was being beaten at his own game. "And what will *you* be doing this Christmas?"

"Spending the morning with my Aunt Ginny and then…" Sam's voice trailed off. She may want to give Flynn MacGregor a Christmas, but in the end, he was still a reporter, and she was still a woman who wanted to keep a few personal details private.

"And then what?"

"I visit other family members."

He studied her. "You don't trust me."

"Should I?"

"Why shouldn't you?"

"Let's be real here, Flynn. You want me for the

story, not for me. And you'll be gone after the holiday. I can't afford to have my heart broken."

"So instead you don't risk it at all."

She met his gaze, seeing in him the same distance that he had maintained from the minute he'd pulled into town. Every once in a while, Flynn had let down his guard—like he had back in the cabin—but most of the time, he had a wall up as unscalable as Alcatraz. "I say what we have here, Mr. MacGregor, is a clear case of the pot calling the kettle black."

He chuckled. "Touché, Miss Barnett." Then he took a step closer, winnowing the gap between them into inches. "Perhaps we should just say goodbye now, rather than delay the inevitable."

"Maybe we should."

"That would be the wisest course."

She didn't move. Didn't breathe. "It would."

"And yet…" He paused. "I'm not leaving."

"You're not?"

"I want what you're offering." A shadow flickered in his eyes, like he'd briefly wandered into a bright room that exposed every vulnerable corner of his soul. "I want a Christmas. Just this once."

Resisting those four words was impossible. Even if it meant opening her heart, being vulnerable and maybe being left alone—and sorry—at the end of all of this.

She'd do it for the boy who hadn't had a Christmas. She'd do it because she saw something in his eyes that bordered on the same longing she had felt ever since Grandma Joy had left.

"I can give you that," Sam whispered. "I can."

Flynn MacGregor had stepped into the one fantasy he'd never allowed himself to have.

A seven-foot Christmas tree stood in the living room, hung with unlit multicolored lights. A string of gold beads draped concentric festive necklaces down the deep green pine branches. Not a single ornament matched. Every one of them, Flynn was sure, from the tiny nutcracker to the delicate gilded bird, was the kind that had a history. A story behind it. An angel held court over the tree, a permanent patient smile on her porcelain face, arms spread wide, as if welcoming Flynn to the room.

Beneath the tree, dozens of wrapped presents waited for tomorrow. For loved ones, for friends. There wasn't one, Flynn knew, for him, but for just a second, he could pretend that this tree was his own. That he would wake up tomorrow in this house and the sun would hit those branches, gilding them with a Christmas morning kiss. That Sam would flick on the tree lights, he would make a wish—

And it would come true.

Damn. He was getting sentimental.

And most of all, forgetting why he had come to this town in the first place.

"I can make some coffee," Sam was saying, "or if you're hungry…"

"Do you have…" He paused. This was insane. He was a reasonable man. A man who never, ever, got emotional. Out of sorts. But something about that tree, that damned tree, had him feeling—

Nostalgic.

Craving things he'd never desired before.

"What?" Sam asked.

Flynn swallowed. Pushed the words past his throat. "Hot chocolate?"

She laughed. "Of course."

He followed her into the kitchen and found this room just as festive as the other. Instead of annoying him, as the town and Betsy's house had when he'd first arrived, Sam's home seemed to wrap him with comfort. Her kitchen, warmly decorated in rich earth tones of russet brown and sage green, held a collection of rustic Santas, marching across the top of the maple cabinets. A quartet of holly-decorated place mats waited for guests at the small oval table, which was ringed with chairs tied with crimson velvet bows. It was beautiful. Picturesque, even.

Oh, boy. He was really getting soft now. Next, he'd be breaking out into song.

Outside the window, a light snow began to fall, the porch light making the white flakes sparkle against the night like tiny stars. Flynn shook his head and let out a soft gust.

"What?" Sam asked, handing him a mug of hot chocolate.

Flynn looked down. Whipped cream curled in an *S* on top of the hot liquid. In a snowman-painted mug. "Of course."

"Of course, what?"

He turned toward her. "It's like you ordered up a Christmas, and it arrived straight out of the catalog, and into your house."

"This? This is nothing. I didn't have enough time this year, because the publicity from that article has kept me so busy at the bakery, to even put up all the decorations. I haven't even turned on the lights once yet. You should see my house when I really—"

He cut off her words with his own mouth, scooping her against him with his free arm. Just as fast, he released her. What had come over him? Every time he turned around, he was kissing her. "Sorry."

"Sorry for kissing me? Was it that bad?"

"No. Not for that." He turned away, heading for the back door. He watched the snow fall and sipped at the hot cocoa. Perfectly chocolately, just the right temperature.

Suddenly, guilt rocketed through him. Here he was, standing in the perfect kitchen, enjoying the perfect cup of hot cocoa, with a woman who could be anyone's wife, when he was far from the kind of man who would make a good husband.

For a moment there, he'd actually pictured himself staying. Enjoying the holiday. Being here, in this crazy town for longer than just one more night.

Who was he kidding? Flynn MacGregor was a nomad. A man who didn't stick, any more than the flakes falling to the ground. In a month or two, or even three, they would melt and be gone, as if they had never existed.

He would be wise to do the same. Instead of thinking he could have what he'd never even dared to dream of.

Especially when this was his last chance to get what he had really come for. What he needed, if he hoped to make that final payment on Liam's tuition, and do what he'd promised Liam he'd do since that day on the beach.

Take care of his brother for as long as he needed him.

Flynn took another sip of hot chocolate, but the drink had lost its sweetness. He shifted position, and something poked him in the chest.

His notepad.

His job. He was supposed to be asking questions. Somehow, he'd lost his compass, forgotten his focus, and Flynn knew exactly when that had happened.

When he'd lost the tight hold on his emotions, let down his guard and kissed Samantha Barnett. He cleared his throat, tugged the notepad and pen from the breast pocket of his jacket and flipped to a clean sheet. Back in work mode, and out of making-mistake mode. Hadn't he learned his lesson back in June? He couldn't afford another mistake like that.

He turned around, back to Sam. "You owe me a few answers, Miss Barnett, remember?"

He worked a smile to his face as he said the words, but he knew Sam caught the no-nonsense tone, the formal name usage. Shadows washed over her features.

Flynn had done what he wanted. He'd erased those kisses, undone them as easily as if he'd painted over the past with a wide brush. Leaving this room, filled with so many rich colors, as pale as an old sheet.

He was so tempted to put the notepad back, to leave the subject alone. Just walk out that door and write a nice, sweet article about a happy baker in the middle of Indiana making cookies that had made dozens of couples fall in love.

And watch his career go right down the toilet.

"Yesterday," he began, clicking his pen on, "I wrote up a draft of my article, and when I finished the piece, I realized there were a few holes."

"Holes?" Sam crossed to the refrigerator, pulled out a selection of cold cuts and condiments, then headed for the breadbox. "Like what?"

"I wanted to ask about your grandmother."

Sam bristled. "I told you. She doesn't work at the bakery anymore."

"Because she lives in a rest home now?"

Her features froze, and a chill whipped through the room. "How do you know about that?"

"This is a small town, like you said. Everyone knows everything." A flicker of regret ran through him. Maybe he shouldn't have said anything. Clearly, this was a subject Sam wanted him to leave untouched.

But he couldn't. Every instinct inside him told him this was where his story lay. If he didn't pursue this line of questioning, he'd surely run his career into the ground.

"I don't want to talk about my grandmother," Sam said. She opened the package of ham, unwrapped a couple slices of cheese, all the while avoiding looking at him.

"She founded the bakery," Flynn said. "She's

where everything began. I think people would want to know—"

Sam wheeled around. "I don't give a damn what people want to know! Let them remember her the way she was, not as this—"

She cut off the words, as if realizing she'd let too much slip already.

"As this invalid who doesn't remember the very dream she helped create?" Flynn finished.

And hated himself.

Tears pooled in Sam's eyes. "Don't. Don't print that."

"It's the truth, Sam. It's—"

"I don't care what it is. I don't care if this is the story that gets you the big headline." She snorted, disgust mixing with the beginnings of tears. "That's all I am to you, isn't it? That's all this was about? A headline?"

"No. That's not it. There's more to this story than that."

"Right." She shook her head. "Tell me you weren't planning on writing some dream falling into a tragedy? Or are you going to pretend that you had something else planned from the beginning? Some happy little piece? I read your articles in the magazine, Flynn, but I kept thinking—" her voice broke and damn, now he really hated himself, really, really did "—you'd be different, that you wouldn't do that to *me*."

The man in Flynn—the one who had kissed Sam, had held her in front of the fire in that cabin—wanted to retreat, to end the conversation before he hit at the raw nerves he knew ran beneath a difficult subject. Hell, he could write the book on raw nerves. And he could see, in Sam's eyes, in the set of her shoulders, that this wasn't something she wanted to talk about. But the reporter in Flynn had to keep going. "I'm not trying to hurt you, Sam. I'm just trying to get to the truth."

Sam wheeled back to face him. "Why? So you can get your headline by dragging my family's personal pain onto the cover? Blasting that news all over town, so people can pity her, pity me? No, I don't think so." Sam slapped the bread onto the counter, twisting off the tie in fast, furious spins, then yanked open the drawer for a butter knife.

Damn. He should have trusted his gut. Should have let this go. But he'd already asked the question, he couldn't retrace those steps. "Trust me, Sam. I'll handle the story nicely. I'll—"

"Trust you? I hardly know you." Sam began to assemble a sandwich, layering ham and cheese, spreading mayonnaise on a slice of bread.

The words slapped him. Although, it seemed like he knew Sam better than he knew anyone in his immediate circle. How could that be? He'd been in this town for a matter of days, and yet, he had shared more with her—and felt as if she had opened up to him—than he had shared in his life.

"Nor do you know my family, or what I've been through," she went on, "so I would appreciate it if you would stick to the cookies, the bakery, and nothing else."

Defensiveness raised the notes in her voice, and maybe if he didn't have someone else depending on him, he would have retreated, would have let the subject drop. But that wasn't the case. And he couldn't afford to let emotion, or sympathy, sway him.

"I need more than just the story of the cookies," Flynn said, deciding he had to push this. He had no time left, and no options. He knew what he had for an article already—and knew what his readers and his editor expected. And it wasn't what Flynn had written. "My editor sent me here to get the whole story, and I'm either getting that, or no story."

"What is that supposed to mean?"

"That I'll go find another bakery to profile in the Valentine's Day issue. You're not the only one baking cookies."

The icy words shattered any remaining warmth between them and Flynn wanted to take them back, but he couldn't. He'd played his trump card, and now it lay heavy in the air between them. Her gaze would have cut him, if it had been a knife.

They had done what he'd expected. Severed the emotional tie.

"You'd seriously do that? Just to get the story?"

"Listen," he said, taking two steps closer, "I'm not here to write some kind of mean-hearted exposé. I know you love your grandmother, I know you want to protect her privacy. But readers want to know what happened to her, too. Heck, the *town* wants to know. Don't you think people worry, care? Want to help?"

"Why? The people who love her already know. That's all that matters."

He moved closer, seeing so much of himself in the way she had closed off the world, insulating herself and her grandmother from everyone else. As if she thought doing so would make it all go away. He knew those walls, knew them so well, he could have told Sam what kind of bricks she'd used to build them. "Did you ever think that maybe people worry and wonder because they care about you, too? That they'll want to help if they know?"

"Help how?" Sam shot back, her voice breaking. She stepped away from him, pacing the kitchen, gesturing with her hands, as if trying to ward off the emotion puddling in her eyes.

"What are they going to do? Send in their best memories to my grandmother, care of the Alzheimer's ward? It's not going to work. She's forgotten me. Forgotten her recipes. Forgotten everything that mattered." Sam turned away, placing a palm against the cabinets, as if seeking strength in the solid wood. "Seeing her is like ripping my own heart out. You tell me why I'd want to share that pain with the rest of America." Her voice broke, the rest of the sentence tearing from her throat. "With *anyone*."

Tears threatened to spill from Sam's emerald eyes. Flynn told himself he didn't care. He told himself that he needed to write down what she'd just said, because they were damned good quotes. Exactly the kind his story needed.

Instead, he dropped the pen to the counter, crossed to Sam and took her in his arms. When he did, it tipped the scales on her emotions, and two tears ran down her cheeks. She remained stiff, unyielding, but he held her tight. "Don't," she whispered. "Don't."

"Okay." And he held her anyway. She cried, and he kept on holding her, her head against his shoulder.

"She doesn't know me," Sam said, her voice muffled, thick. "She doesn't know who I am."

"And you're carrying this all by yourself."

"I have my aunt Ginny."

"Sam," Flynn said, his voice warm against her hair, "that's not sharing the burden, not really. And you know it. You carry this bakery, this house, your grandmother, all on your shoulders. Why?"

She turned away, spinning out of his arms, crossing back to the sandwiches, but she didn't pick up the knife or top the ham with a slice of bread. She just gripped the countertop like a life preserver. "Because I have to. Because if I rely on anyone else…"

Her voice trailed off, fading into the heavy silence of the kitchen.

And then Flynn knew, knew as well as he knew the back of his own hand, what the answer was. Because Sam was him, in so many ways. His heart broke for her, and he wished he could do something, anything to ease her pain. But Flynn MacGregor couldn't fix Sam's situation any more than he could fix his own. "Because if you rely on anyone else, they might let you down."

"I…" She stopped, caught her breath. "Yes."

He let out a half laugh. "We're two of a kind, aren't we? Neither one of us wants to put our trust in other people, just in case things don't last. Only, you have more faith than me."

"Me?"

"You still live in the fairy tale," Flynn said, waving at her kitchen, at the Christmas paradise that surrounded them. "And I…I gave up on that a long time ago."

"You don't have to, Flynn. It still exists."

"Maybe for you," he said, a smile that felt bitter crossing his face. "You can reach out, to the town, you can lean on other people, and you can try to connect with your grandmother, and try to build that bridge."

"How am I supposed to do that?" She swiped at her face, brushing away the remaining tears. "Last time I went there, she thought I was the maid."

Flynn might not be able to fix everything for Sam, but he could help with this. A little. Maybe. "This fall I did a story on a chef whose wife had Alzheimer's," he said. "It was heartbreaking for him, because the restaurant, everything, had always been all about her. His whole life was about her. When I interviewed him, he didn't want to talk about the restaurant at all. He only wanted to tell me about this photo album he was making. It had all the moments of their life. From the day they met through the day their kids were born, through every day they spent in the restaurant. He'd go over to her room, every single afternoon and flip through that book. It didn't bring her back all the way, but there were days, he said, when she would look at him, and know him."

Sam glanced up at him. "Really?"

Flynn nodded. Even now, months after writing the story, it still moved his heart, and tightened his chest. He remembered that man, the tender way he'd loved his wife, as if it were yesterday. *That* had been the kind of article Flynn wanted to write, but it wasn't what he'd ended up writing.

Instead, he'd done the kind of piece he'd always done. A story on how a dream had died, along with the woman's memories, and the man's inattention, because he wasn't at the restaurant as often as he should be. Because he was with his wife.

How would it have felt to write the other story? The kind he'd written a few days ago in the back of Sam's shop?

Sam's gaze, still watery, met his. "And what kind of story will you write about me? One as sweet as what you just told me?"

He swallowed hard. What could he tell her? The truth would hurt, and lying would only delay the inevitable. So he just didn't answer at all.

"Thanks for the hot chocolate," Flynn said, placing the mug on the counter before it got too comfortable in his grasp. "But I have to go."

Then he grabbed his coat and headed out the door. Because the one thing he couldn't do was break Samantha Barnett's heart on Christmas Eve.

CHAPTER FIFTEEN

"MERRY CHRISTMAS," Sam whispered, pressing a kiss to her grandmother's cheek.

Joy stirred, then swung her gaze over to Sam's. "Is it Christmas?"

Sam nodded, then pulled up the chair beside her grandmother's bed and took a seat. On the opposite side of the room, Grandma Joy's roommate snored loudly, under a red-and-green plaid blanket. Sam reached for her grandmother's hand, then pulled back, not wanting to scare her by becoming too familiar too quickly. "Yes, it's Christmas."

"Oh, that's my favorite day of the year." Joy sat up in the bed, pushing her short white hair out of her eyes.

"I know." Sam smiled. God, how she missed those days, when her grandmother would decorate the house and pour every ounce of energy into making the holiday merry. The house would ring with the sound of singing, the halls would be filled with the scents of baking. Both generations of Barnett woman had loved Christmas, and passed that holiday spirit on to Sam. "They're having a piano player come today, to play for everyone here. For the holiday party."

Her grandmother smiled. "That will be nice."

"Do you want me to help you get ready?"

"Of course. I'll want to look my prettiest for the party."

Sam tried to keep her spirits up, to not let the lack of recognition dampen her Christmas, but every year she came to Heritage Nursing Home and every year, it seemed to be the same story. There had been holidays, in the beginning, before the Alzheimer's had gotten so bad that her grandmother had to be hospitalized, when Joy would remember, but then, it seemed as if the entire world became strange, and though Sam kept praying for a miracle, for a window to open, if only briefly—

It didn't.

But was it possible, Sam wondered, as Flynn had told her, to help push that window open? For a long time, Sam had tried, by bringing in her grandmother's favorite things from home, and hanging pictures of loved ones around the room, but then she'd given up, frustrated and depressed. Maybe it was time she tried again. In a bigger way than ever before.

"I brought you a gift," Sam said.

"For me?" Grandma Joy smiled. "Thank you."

Sam held her breath and put the wrapped package into her grandmother's hands. What if Flynn had been wrong? What if this was the worst idea ever?

Joy removed the bow, smiling over the fancy gold-and-white fabric decoration, then undid the bright, holiday packaging. She ran a hand over the leather album. "A book?"

"Of sorts. It's a story." Sam swallowed. "About you. And…" She took in a breath. "Me."

"Us?" Confusion knitted Grandma Joy's brows. She looked down again at the thick brown cover, then opened the book and began to turn the pages.

Page after page, Joy and Sam's lives flashed by in a series of images. A young Joy working at the bakery with her husband in the first few days after it opened. More pictures of her, as a new mother, with baby Emma in her arms, then handing out baked goods at a church fund-raiser, then, at Emma's wedding. Joy paused when she reached the picture of herself holding a newborn Sam, her face beaming with pride. Her fingers drifted lightly over the image of her grandbaby. "So beautiful," she whispered.

Sam could only nod. This was too painful. Flynn had been wrong. How could she possibly sit here and watch her grandmother not remember the most important days of her life?

Joy turned another page, to images of Sam in kindergarten, then the second-grade class play, then to older pictures of Sam, after her parents had died and she had gone to live just with her grandparents. Middle school science fair, high school awards nights, and so many pictures of Sam working with Joy at the bakery, others at church on Easter, in front of Christmas trees. Joy paused, over and over again, mute, simply tracing over the pictures, her fingers dancing down faces.

Sam shifted in her chair. She was tempted to leave. She couldn't watch this for one more second. She half rose, opening her mouth to say goodbye, when her grandmother reached out a hand.

"This one, do you remember it?"

Sam dropped back down. "Do I remember…?" She leaned forward and looked into the album. It was one of the last pictures of her and her grandmother, before her grandmother had been admitted to Heritage Nursing Home. They stood together, arm in arm, in front of the bakery, beaming. Still a team then, thinking they'd run things together. A good day, one of the few Joy had had left. "Yes."

"My sister Ginny took the picture."

Sam's breath caught in her throat. "Yes, she did." Six months before everything had changed, when Aunt Ginny had come up for a visit, not realizing that things would get so bad so fast later and Sam would be forced into taking over the bakery, but Sam didn't mention that part. There were certain things she was glad her grandmother had forgotten.

Her grandmother smiled. "It's a beautiful picture."

Sam exhaled, deflating like a balloon. "Yeah. It is." And now she did rise, tears clogging her throat, burning her eyes. She couldn't spend another Christmas being mistaken for a stranger. Her heart hurt too much.

This was why she couldn't stay in Riverbend. This was why she couldn't give her heart to anyone else. Because she didn't have it in her to see it fall apart, crumble so easily. Not again.

"It's so beautiful," Grandma Joy repeated, "just like my granddaughter." She reached out a hand—long, graceful fingers exactly like Sam's—and grasped Sam's wrist before Sam could walk away. She stared at Sam, for a long, long time, then she smiled, her eyes lighting in a way Sam hadn't seen them brighten in so, so long. "Just like you, Samantha."

"Did you…did you just say my name?" Sam asked.

"Of course. You're my granddaughter, aren't you?"

Sam nodded, mute, tears spilling over, blurring her vision. She sank down again, this time onto the soft mattress, and reached out, drawing her grandmother into one more hug.

And when Grandma Joy's arms went around her, fierce and tight, Samantha Barnett started believing in Christmas miracles again.

Betsy was singing.

If Flynn didn't know better, he'd have sworn a cow was dying in the front parlor of the bed and breakfast. He headed downstairs on Christmas morning, going straight for the coffeepot. In the parlor, the few remaining guests were gathered around the piano, joining Betsy in a rousing and agonizingly off-key rendition of "O Little Town of Bethlehem."

From the dining room, Flynn watched the group. He stood on the periphery, never more aware he was on the outside. How long had he lived like this? Outside of normal people's lives?

Living another kind of normal. One that he now realized was far from normal.

The front door to Betsy's opened and Sam walked in, her arms laden with boxes from the bakery. Flynn put down his coffee and hurried over to help her. "I thought you were under Doctor Earl's orders not to work on Christmas Eve."

"I baked these ahead of time. And besides, it's not Christmas Eve anymore, it's Christmas Day. So merry Christmas." She gave him a smile.

A smile? After the way things had ended between them yesterday? Flynn didn't question the facial gesture, but wondered. Why the change?

"But you *are* working, even on Christmas?" he said.

"I'm delivering, not working." She thought about it for a second. "Okay, yes. But only for a little while. And, I had an ulterior motive."

He unpacked a box of Danishes, laying them in a concentric circle on a silver-plated platter. It reminded him of the first time he'd done this, right after arriving in town. That seemed like a hundred years ago, as if he'd met Sam a lifetime ago. Before yesterday, he'd thought...

Thought maybe there was a chance they could have something. What that something could be, he wasn't sure, because he lived on the East Coast and she lived in the Midwest, and their worlds were as opposite as the North and South Poles.

And then he'd gone and driven a wedge between them yesterday. Had made it clear where his priorities lay—with his job.

If there'd been another choice, Flynn would have grabbed it in a second. Another choice...

He looked at Sam, her face bright and happy,

her hair seeming like gold above the red sweater she wore, and wished for a miracle. It was Christmas, after all. Maybe a miracle would come along.

Uh-huh. And maybe Santa would just sweep on through the front door, too. Best to abandon that train of thought before it derailed his plans to leave.

"Ulterior motive?" he asked.

"You left last night before I could give you your Christmas gift."

That drew Flynn up short. "You bought me a *Christmas gift*?"

"Well, I had to sort of improvise, and your gift is, ah—" she looked at her watch "—not quite here yet, because what I bought you is still in my Jeep, which is on the side of the road."

"You bought me a gift yesterday?" He couldn't have been more surprised if Santa himself had marched in and handed him a present.

"Of course. It's Christmas. Everyone should have a gift on Christmas. I was going to give it before you—"

Even though he knew he shouldn't, even though he'd just vowed a half second ago to stay away from her, Flynn surged forward, cupped her face with both his hands and kissed her. "Thank you."

She laughed. "You don't even know what I got you. You could hate it."

"It doesn't matter. It's the thought that counts." She had thought of him. Thought about whether he would have a merry Christmas. Who had worried about his Christmas? Ever? Flynn couldn't remember anyone ever doing that. Most holiday seasons, he and Liam had been between homes, shuffled off by the system to some emergency place, a temporary landing, before they'd be off to the next family. But no one had latched on to the boys who rebelled, who didn't connect, fit in with their little blond-haired boys and girls.

The fact that Sam, a woman he had met a few days ago, would go to so much trouble, for him, blasted against him.

He might not be a little kid anymore, and no longer cared if there was a gift under the tree, or heck, a tree in his living room, but to know that someone had taken the time to plan a gift like that…

It touched him more than he had thought possible.

A fierce longing tugged at him, and the urge to leave dissipated. Instead, he found himself wanting to stay. Here, in this town. This crazy, Christmas-frantic town.

"Are you speaking in trite phrases now, Flynn MacGregor?"

"I, ah, think this town is rubbing off on me."

Sam laughed again. "You must be catching pneumonia or something."

"I've caught something," Flynn said, tracing Sam's lips with his fingertips. Wanting to kiss her again. Wanting to do much more than that, but painfully aware that they were in Betsy's dining room.

"Come on in, Flynn, Sam!" Betsy called. "And join us!"

Sam's eyes danced with a dare. "Are you feeling truly festive?"

He cringed. "Singing with Betsy might be pushing it."

Sam grabbed one of his hands and pulled him toward the parlor. "It'll be good for you, Flynn."

And as he stood by the piano a moment later with an assortment of strangers, his arm wrapped around Sam's waist, joining in on "Jingle Bells," a swell of holiday spirit started in Flynn's chest and began to grow, as if the music itself was pounding Christmas right into him. Somehow, he seemed to know the words, or at least snippets of them, to every song. Perhaps he'd absorbed them over the years, some kind of holiday osmosis, and he added his baritone to the rest of the singers. Sam leaned her head against his shoulder, and for those moments, everything seemed completely perfect in Flynn's world.

A truth whispered in his ear, one he wasn't prepared to hear.

He loved this woman.

Loved her. It didn't matter that it had happened in four days, four weeks or four years. The feeling ran so deep, and so strong, Flynn could no longer ignore it.

For the first time in his life, he wanted depth, he wanted a real relationship, no more convenience dating, the kind of flighty relationship he'd had with Mimi. She was surely off in some foreign country, probably flirting with someone else, which didn't bother Flynn one bit.

He had everything he wanted right here with him.

Never before had he fallen in love, but he recognized the emotion as clearly as his own name. His arm tightened around Sam's waist, and he vowed that as soon as the song ended, he would pull Sam aside and tell her.

Another set of chimes joined in with the piano. It took a moment for anyone to realize the sound was coming from the doorbell, and not Betsy's feet. "Oh, someone's here," Betsy said. "I hope whoever it is, sings tenor!"

"I'll get it," Flynn said, releasing Sam to cross the front parlor, head into the hall and down to the door. He expected one of the guest's relatives. Or maybe Earl, here to chide Sam about making a delivery on Christmas Day.

But when Flynn pulled open the door, he found

a gift no one could have fit under a tree. And one he wasn't so sure was glad to be here.

His brother.

"What are you doing here?"

"I was invited," Liam said. He picked up a suitcase that had been sitting by his feet. A suitcase? Why? Was he intending to stay a while?

Confusion waged a war in Flynn's gut. Who had called Liam? Why? And what had made Liam drive all the way up here?

The tension between them ran as thick as syrup. Flynn knew the choice was his. He could step aside, let Liam pass and leave the moment as it was, or he could do something about it.

Liam hoisted the suitcase higher in his grip and moved forward, making the decision for him. Before his younger brother could pass, Flynn reached out and drew Liam into a tight embrace. "Hi, Liam."

Liam stiffened, then patted Flynn's back in a gesture meant more for a stranger than a relative. "Hi, Flynn."

Damn, how he had missed his brother. It didn't matter if two years or two minutes had passed, whether they were in their twenties or still in elementary school. A fierce love rose in Flynn's chest, and he held tight for a long moment, his mind whipping back to the beach, to the two of them together against the wind, swearing to always be together. Always.

Flynn clapped his brother hard on the back, then released him. He swept his gaze over Liam, who was thinner than Flynn remembered, but still had the same tall, dark good looks. His hair was curlier, his eyes tended more toward green than blue, but otherwise, the two shared a lot of the same characteristics. "It's good to see you."

Really good.

"Yeah. Same to you." Liam came inside and shut the door behind him, then dropped the suitcase to the floor. Behind them, the caroling continued, segueing into "We Wish You a Merry Christmas." Liam shuffled from foot to foot, ran a hand through his hair. "Singing, huh?"

"Yeah."

Some more silence extended between them. If one of them didn't say something, Flynn knew they never would. There'd been too many phone calls, too many visits, that had been filled with awkward small talk and anguished pauses, and nothing of substance. He cleared his throat. "Listen, Liam, about the last time we saw each other—"

"You don't have to say anything."

"Yeah, I do." Flynn ran a hand over his face, then met his brother's gaze. "All I've been trying to do is take care of you. But you make it damned hard sometimes."

Liam shook his head, and a flush of frustration rose in his cheeks. "Flynn, I'm all grown up now. I can take care of myself."

"I know, but…" Flynn let out a breath.

"There's no buts. You keep on trying to throw money at me. I don't want that, Flynn. I want—" Liam cut off his sentence and let out a low curse.

"You want what?" Flynn prompted when Liam didn't continue. Behind them, the group had moved onto "O Little Town of Bethlehem."

Liam stared at his shoes for a long while, then finally looked up and met Flynn's gaze. "I want you, big brother. Not your damned money."

There. It was out. The truth. Liam needed the one thing Flynn had always held back, kept tucked away. His heart. His emotions.

And what good had it done him? Left him alone, estranged from his brother, living one holiday after another without anyone.

Flynn ran a hand along the woodwork, fingers tracing the thick oak. "I was wrong, Liam. I pushed you away…."

"Because I was a reminder of all we went through," Liam said, finishing the sentence.

"Yeah." Here he'd thought he'd been control- ling his life. Controlling his emotions. When all he'd done was shove them in a closet and ignore them.

Liam's gaze met his older sibling's. In that moment, a shared history unfurled between them, a mental *This is Your Life*, that played in an instant, then came around full circle to the two of them, together then, together now. "Yeah, me, too."

There was no need for words, no need for anything other than that assent. They knew, because they'd been there. Because they shared the same DNA. And heck, because they were guys. Blubbering for hours simply wasn't the way they handled things.

Flynn reached out, and drew his brother to him again, in an even tighter embrace this time, one that lasted longer, and made up for the last two years. "Merry Christmas, Liam."

Flynn couldn't hear his brother's response, because he was holding him too tight. But it didn't matter. He didn't need to hear the words to know his little brother felt the same.

Because this time, Liam hugged him back.

"Oh, we have another guest!" Betsy exclaimed from behind them. "At Betsy's Bed and Breakfast—"

"There's always room for one more," Flynn finished for her.

Betsy grinned. "Absolutely!"

Flynn picked up his brother's suitcase. "Come on in, make yourself at home."

Liam gave Flynn a dubious glance, as he watched Betsy hurry forward, her house slippers jingle-jangling, her mouth going nonstop about the town, the Christmas activities planned for the day, the dinner menu, the local call policy. "Is it always like this here?"

"Yep. And that's the beauty of the place. Hang around for the Christmas carols," Flynn said. "They're the best part."

Liam glanced over at him, eyes wide. Flynn just laughed, and it felt damned good to do so.

CHAPTER SIXTEEN

SAM SLIPPED OUT Betsy's back door. She'd seen Flynn greet his brother and knew she had done what she wanted to do. She had given Flynn the merry Christmas she had intended.

The wind stung her face as soon as she stepped outside, and at first, she couldn't understand why the cold hurt so bad, until she realized her cheeks were covered with tears, and winter's wrath had turned them to ice. She swiped at her face with her glove, then walked the few blocks to the bakery, opting for the peace of the shop, instead of heading to Aunt Ginny's house.

She let herself inside Joyful Creations, turning on a single light. Then she headed to the case, filled a plate with all the treats she never had time to eat, put on a pot of coffee, and when it was ready, she took her snack out to one of the café tables, as if she were a customer.

She sat down, and for the first time in a long

time, enjoyed the fruits of her labor. Outside the window, a soft snow began to fall, a dusting, really, just enough to sparkle for the holiday.

The door opened and Earl poked his head in. "What on earth are you doing, Sam? It's Christmas."

She smiled. "I could say the same to you."

"I'm on my way over to Betsy's. I've got her Christmas gift out here."

"Out there?" Sam rose out of her chair and peeked through the window. "You bought her a truck?"

"Hell no. I bought her what's in the back of my truck." Earl beamed with pride at his thoughtfulness. "A new washer machine."

"Oh. How romantic."

"My Betsy is practical. She's gonna love it. You'll see." He adjusted his hat, then gave Sam another disapproving glance. "You aren't planning on spending your holiday in here, now are you?"

"No. I'm going to my Aunt Ginny's."

"Good. You need to do more for yourself. You don't want to make this place your life, Sam. We need you around this town more than we need a bakery." He tipped his head toward her to emphasize the point. "If you see Joy today at that fancy retirement place, please give her my best. I sure do miss seeing her 'round here."

Sam drew in a breath. Flynn was right. It was time to tell the people of this town about Grandma Joy. Everyone in Riverbend cared about her—hadn't they made that obvious a hundred times over? And they'd cared about her grandmother, and would continue to care—regardless of what had happened, and whether Grandma remembered them or not. "No, Earl. My grandmother doesn't live in a retirement village. She never did." Sam paused. "Grandma Joy lives at Heritage Nursing Home, in the Alzheimer's unit."

Earl looked at her in shock for a long moment, then he nodded somberly, as if he'd expected to hear that. "I saw her mind going, long time ago. I wondered how long it would be. I'm sorry, Sam. But you made the right decision." He ambled into the store, and gave her a hug.

Sam's heart filled, the love of the people of Riverbend bursting in her chest. "Thanks, Earl." She brushed away a few tears, but this time, they weren't tears of sorrow, just tears of gratitude for the comfort of others.

"Don't think nothing of it. Maybe me and Betsy, we'll head on over there, see her today."

"She probably won't remember you."

Earl waved a hand in dismissal. "That's okay. Half the time I don't remember my own name." He grinned. "And if your grandma doesn't know me, it won't bother me none. Why, it'll be like making a new friend every time I go up there."

After a final warning not to work all day, Earl wished her a merry Christmas then headed out the door. Sam watched him go, feeling lighter than she had in a long time. Flynn had been right. Sharing the burden suddenly made it a lot easier to bear.

Now if she could only find a way to have it all—a life and carry on her grandmother's legacy, she'd be all set. Sam sighed, then took Earl's advice, and turned out the lights.

Flynn paused on Sam's doorstep, shifting the scratchy gift in his hands to his opposite arm. He rang the bell and waited. What if she wasn't home? What if she'd gone to her aunt's house? What if—

But then the door opened and Sam stood on the other side, a roll of wrapping paper in one hand. "Flynn."

"You're still here. I thought you might have gone to your aunt's already."

She held up the wrapping paper. "Working too much, not enough time to wrap gifts. So, I'm running late. What are you doing here?"

"I came here to say Merry Christmas."

"Merry Christmas, Flynn." A smile crossed her lips. "I think we already had this conversation this morning."

"It worked pretty well the first time, didn't it?" He grinned. "This is for you. It's, ah, not much, because there's not exactly many shopping options on Christmas Day, and yesterday's shopping trip was ended prematurely."

She laid the wrapping paper against the door, then took the wreath from his hands, the smile on her face widening. "A Christmas wreath?"

"I noticed you didn't have one on your front door. There was this guy selling them on the corner of Main this morning, and when I saw them, I—"

"*You* noticed I didn't have a wreath?"

"Is that so unusual?"

She hung the wreath on her front door, straightened the red velvet bow, then turned back to him, shutting the door behind her. "For one, you're a guy. For another, of everyone in town—"

"I had the least Christmas spirit."

"Well, yeah." She arched a brow. "Had?"

Flynn crossed to Sam, taking her hands in his. "I changed my mind about the holiday."

"What changed your mind?"

"Well, it sure wasn't Betsy's singing. Or her jingle bell slippers." He grinned. "It was you."

"Me? How could I do that?"

He reached up and cupped her jaw, tracing her bottom lip with his thumb. "Thank you for bringing my brother here. When you did that, you showed me what was important. That I had my priorities as backward as a man could get them."

Confusion warred in her green eyes.

"I wrote my article early this morning, and sent it in to my editor. Turns out one of the guests at Betsy's had a national broadband connection on his laptop, and we got it to work by sitting in the backyard, freezing our butts off." He chuckled. "Doesn't matter. The article is done, and gone. No going back. But I still wanted you to read it. Either way, no matter what happens, I'm not changing a word."

Her face fell, and she stepped away. "Just be kind, Flynn. That's all I ask."

He fished the papers he'd printed that morning on his portable printer out of his pocket and handed them to Sam. "Read it, and then judge, Sam."

She took the sheaf of pages, then turned away from him, crossing into the living room. She sank onto one of the sofas, flicked on a lamp and began to read.

Flynn already knew the words on the page. It hadn't been all that hard to recall them from the first draft. His heart had committed those earlier pages to memory, and when he'd sat down to write, the article had poured from him, as easily as water from a faucet. *Visions of sugar plums dance…*

Long minutes passed, without Sam saying a word. She read, turning the pages slowly, while Flynn's breath held, his lungs tight. Finally, she looked up, her green eyes watery.

Damn. Had he written the piece wrong? Had he, despite his best intentions, still ruined everything?

"Flynn. It's—" she drew in a breath, searching for words "—wonderful."

He exhaled. "It's not what my editor wants. Or what my readers expect. It's not, in fact, at all what I was paid to write. I'll probably be fired." He grinned. "So if you're looking for a little help making cookies…I might need a job on the twenty-sixth."

"But…why? Why would you do this?"

He crossed to the sofa and sat down beside her. "I realized that my career didn't matter if it cost me peace of mind. Happiness." He drew in a breath. "Happiness with you, Sam, because…I love you."

Her eyes widened. "You love me?"

Flynn felt a goofy grin take over his face, the kind that made his jaw go slack with happiness. "Yes. I do. And I know it sounds crazy because I've only known you for a matter of days, but one of those days was spent stuck in a cabin in the woods, so that's like triple time, because we were alone so much, and—"

She surged forward, the papers on her lap falling to the floor, and kissed him. "Oh, Flynn. I love you, too."

Joy exploded in his chest. She loved him, too. Holy cow. This was what other men felt when a woman said those words? This was what made them settle down, have kids, buy a house in the suburbs? No wonder.

And what the heck had he been doing all this time, denying himself this? Thinking he was happier alone?

"All my life," he said, "I've controlled my emotions, held them back, because I thought it was easier not to feel, not to open my heart to other people—"

"Because protecting your heart kept it from getting it hurt," Sam finished. "But in the end, all it did was leave you alone. And unhappy."

He nodded. He placed a hand against her cheek, seeing so much of himself in her eyes. "You did the same thing."

"And got the same result." She worked a smile to her face, but it fell flat. "I don't want to be alone anymore, Flynn."

Flynn opened his arms, and drew Sam against his chest. "You won't be, Sam. And neither will I."

They held each other for a long time, while the snow fell softly outside, and the fire crackled in the fireplace. In all his life, Flynn could have never imagined a Christmas gift as wonderful as this.

Sam drew back, her gaze going over Flynn's shoulder. "I forgot to turn on the lights for the Christmas tree." She rose, pulling Flynn up with her, and they crossed to the seven-foot spruce.

Flynn ran a hand down the tree, his touch skipping over the history of Sam's life contained in the dozens and dozens of ornaments. Someday, he'd know the story behind every one of these. Because he would be with her for next Christmas and the one after that, and they would hang these ornaments together. He could hear her telling him that her grandmother had baked those salt dough gingerbread men, and her Aunt Ginny had made those macramé birds. That she'd bought the cable car on a trip to San Francisco, found the pinecone on a long hike in the woods. The joy in his heart tripled, for the future he could finally see, one with Sam by his side.

"Here," Sam said, handing him a switch. "You can do it. And don't forget to make a wish."

Flynn smiled. "I don't need to. My wish already came true." He pressed the button for the lights into Sam's palm. "You make the wish."

She closed her eyes, whispered a few words, then pressed the button. The lights came on, illuminating the tree with a burst of tiny white lights.

A second later, they began to blink in a synchronized dance. "My favorite moment," she said. "The first time. It's like that's when Christmas really starts."

"What did you wish for?"

"If I tell you," she said, grinning, "it might not come true."

"If you wished for me to marry you," Flynn replied, swinging Sam back into his arms, "then that's one wish that's going to come true, because there's no way I'm letting you get away, Samantha Barnett."

Surprise arched her brows again. "You move fast, Flynn MacGregor."

"There's another thing you should know about me. When I see something I want, I go after it."

She smiled, then a moment passed, and the smile fell from her face. "I can't marry you, Flynn. It wouldn't be fair to you."

"What do you mean, it wouldn't be fair? We can find a way to make anything work, Sam."

"Do you want to know what I wished for?" She leaned her head against his chest. Flynn inhaled, catching the scent of sugar cookies. For the rest of his life, he'd associate that scent with Sam. "I wished for a way to have everything I wanted."

"I'm not enough?" He chuckled.

She looked up at him, sorrow filling her gaze. "I can't afford to pay for the treatment my grandmother needs, not without expanding Joyful Creations beyond the bounds of Riverbend. To expand, I have to work more hours. And if I'm working more hours, I won't be much of a wife, or a mother, if we ever have children."

Children. He hadn't thought of having kids—had never pictured himself with his own children at all—but now that Sam had said the word, he realized he did want a family.

A big family. A dog. A house. The whole enchilada.

But Sam was right. She couldn't have a life, and run multiple locations, not in such a demanding field. Hadn't he seen that when he'd went to live at Mondo's house? The chef and his wife had never been home, and eventually, called children's services to give back the foster children they'd taken in. Their best intentions had been undone by a work schedule that didn't allow for a family. He'd heard the same story over and over again. So many families tried to make it work, but in an industry that required early mornings and late nights, it was almost impossible. Some could work it out, but so many were forced to choose between business and home.

And as for Sam, if she had more than one location, along with the demands that came with those early years of still building her business?

He didn't see how she could have it all, either. Not unless…

"What if there was another way to expand Joyful Creations beyond Riverbend?" he said.

"Another way? What are you talking about?"

"It would require having Internet service," Flynn said with a grin. "Reliable postal service."

"Now *that* we have."

"Good." The idea exploded in his head, all those years of covering the food industry, and learning from chefs and experts coalescing at once. "What if you started a Web site? To sell, not just the regular cookies and desserts, but also the 'love cookies'? They already have a national reputation, and once my article runs—"

"I thought you said your editor would hate it."

"If he does, I'll just sell it somewhere else. It's a good article, Sam. A damned good article. I'll sell it, and in the process, make Joyful Creations even more famous."

"Ship the cookies. And stay here." Sam thought about that, pacing as she talked aloud. "It could work. I wouldn't have to move away from my grandmother or my aunt, and if I needed to increase production, I could always rent more space from the shop next door. They have a back room they don't use. My overhead would be low, the hours I'd have to put in…" She spun back toward him. "It could work."

"And you could have it all, Sam. Stay here, have a family." He grinned. "Have me, if you want."

"Of course I do." She crossed back to him, slipping into his arms as if she had always been there, fitting as easily as a link in a chain. "You're part of the package, Flynn MacGregor."

He leaned down and kissed her, capturing the taste of vanilla, the scent of cinnamon, the sweetness of Sam. Everything he'd ever wanted, in one beautiful, wonderful Christmas gift. "You know what people are going to say, don't you?"

"Hmm…what?"

"That we fell in love because of those cookies."

"But we never even ate any."

"No one knows if we did or not. And if it's rumored that we did…"

Sam grinned. "It'll be good for business."

"As long as it's good for us, I'm okay with that." Then Flynn kissed the woman he loved again, while the lights from the tree cast their golden light on her face. For the first time in his life, Flynn MacGregor believed in Santa Claus, because the jolly man had finally listened and given him the perfect gift.

The *only* gift he'd ever really wanted for Christmas—

A home.

Christmas is a special time for family...

...and two handsome single fathers are looking for wives!

The Christmas Baby by Eve Gaddy

Comfort and Joy by Amy Frazier

Available 21st November 2008

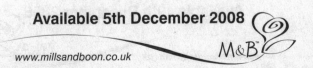

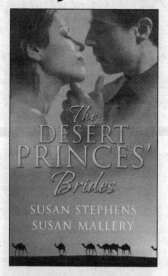